The rest of his da
had no more dead pe
and didn't really wan
bachelor pad above the practice just y...
at the clock confirmed it was nearly seven p.m. Ben grabbed the phone and dialed the number quickly, before he could change his mind.

It rang twice before Tim picked up, sounding a little out of breath. "Hello?"

"Oh, hi. Sorry, I didn't mean to interrupt anything. I mean. Hi. This is Ben Sauvigon. The vet from this afternoon?" God, he was a dork.

He heard Tim laugh softly, though it didn't sound rude. "You're still there, too. I have Caller ID. And you're not interrupting anything, I was just working out."

Okay, he so didn't need the image of a half-naked, sweaty man doing crunches. Well, he loved the image, but it wasn't doing anything for his composure. "Yeah, I... I haven't eaten yet, I was wondering if you had?"

"Not yet, no." There was a pause and Ben could swear he heard Tim drinking, gulping water or something. "But I'm starving. Do you have anything in mind?"

"I was going to just pick up some Chinese from around the corner. I live above the practice."

"Yeah? Chinese sounds good. I need to shower real fast."

Once Upon a Veterinarian
TOP SHELF
Copyright © 2008 Drew Zachary
An imprint of Torquere Press Publishers
PO Box 2545
Round Rock, TX 78680
Cover illustration by Alessia Brio
Published with permission
ISBN: 978-1-60370-494-6, 1-60370-494-9
www.torquerepress.com

**If you enjoyed Once Upon a Veterinarian,
you might enjoy these Torquere Press titles:**

Catching a Second Wind by Sean Michael

Drawing Closer by Jane Davitt

On Fire by Drew Zachary

The Painted House by Drew Zachary

Riding Heartbreak Road by Kiernan Kelly

Once Upon a Veterinarian

Once Upon a Veterinarian
by Drew Zachary

Torquere
Press
Inc.
romance for the rest of us
www.torquerepress.com

Once Upon a Veterinarian

Chapter One

Ben gathered Miss Fluffy up and carried her over to little Suzie-Ann, putting the huge Himalayan into the little girl's arms. Then he crouched down so he was eye to eye with Suzie-Ann. "She's still a little groggy, so you need to keep her in her carry-case when you get her home, and put her in a room where the dog can't bother her, okay?"

Big blue eyes looked solemnly into his own and Suzie-Ann nodded.

"Did your mother bring her carrier?"

He got another nod.

"Good. She'll be just fine, sweetie. By tomorrow she'll be back to her old self." He stood and watched Suzie-Ann carry the cat over to her mother, who was waiting by the door with the carrier in hand. Excellent.

He put a check by Miss Fluffy's name on his mental list and let himself forget about her. Just as well; she was a mean, old, flat-faced feline who had very little time or patience for anyone but the little girl who owned her.

His partner, Stacey, was restocking her bag. She looked tired. Even her fiery red curls didn't seem to bounce like they usually did. Of course, it was calving season, and she was out at least once a night to help one cow or another to deliver.

"You should try for a nap when you're finished with that."

"Yeah, that'd be good. Tell it to the cows, Benji." She pushed her hair back with one hand and stood up with a groan. "I'll sleep next month. Maybe."

He shook his head. He didn't know where she got the energy.

There was just the two of them at the practice, a couple of nurses, and one tech. He did small animals; his petite partner specialized in farm animals. They were both on call a lot, the joys of having your own business, but his sleep was disturbed far less than hers was.

He sat, lanky frame folding down into the waiting-room-style chair. "I had another poisoning today. That's the third cat this week."

Stacey froze and turned slowly to face him full on. "That makes... what? Six in total? It's time to call in the police, Ben. It's criminal. They have to listen now. Did the latest one die?"

He nodded, remembering the sad faces of a pair of twin boys. "Kat wasn't even an outdoor animal, but apparently he liked sneaking out when they weren't looking. I'm wondering if Mrs. Pool's dog, Corky, wasn't also a poisoning." He sighed and scrubbed at his face. Dying pets were the hardest part of this job, but for someone to have deliberately poisoned them... Well, Stacey was right. It was criminal.

"Call," she said as she picked up her bag. "Today. And make sure you have the lab results to show them, too. Cops tend to like lab results. I'll be out at Richardson's if you need me, okay?"

He looked at his watch and nodded. He had ten

minutes or so before his next appointment. More than enough time to call and get his paperwork on the dead animals together. "Your cell phone actually charged up today?"

"I think so?" She didn't sound sure. "Try it and find out. If not, the barn line is in our files." She didn't look even vaguely bothered to have no idea about her phone.

He shook his head. He wasn't going to bother trying the cell; it was either working or it wasn't. It wasn't like she could charge it up before she left anyway. "Make sure you save me some of whatever Mrs. Richardson gives you."

"Hey. Those are *my* muffins and cookies, dude. You want some, you stick your arm up a cow and help it birth."

"Oh, I don't think so. We share in the profits from both sides of the practice and, in my books, that includes the goodies." It wasn't *his* fault that they were more likely to get goodies from the farm visits than they did from the clinic clients he tended to.

"Your books are wrong." She smiled sweetly at him and went to the door, leaning on it to push it open so she could get out. "Call the police. Leave me a note or something to fill me in, okay?"

"Yeah, okay. Go make babies happen." He gave her a wink and headed for his office, passing the reception area on the way. "Amy? I've got a call to make, but you can send Jason and Beastly in to the exam room."

"Yes, Dr. Sauvigon."

Ben grabbed a coffee on the way, and a mini powdered sugar doughnut. He popped it into his mouth, immediately wishing he'd picked up more than one -- they were tiny. Settled at his desk, Ben pulled out the phonebook, looking up the non-emergency number for the police. He didn't figure they were going to be very happy about having to send someone out to talk to him about dead cats, but this wasn't an anomaly or accidental garden fertilizer poisoning anymore. This was serious.

He dialed the phone and cleared his throat, ready with the grave voice he usually reserved for telling clients their pets had just died.

He just hoped the cops would take it seriously.

Constable Tim Geary of the Ontario Provincial Police took his time getting to the Terry Road Veterinary Clinic. It wasn't like he needed lights and sirens to take a statement, after all. He was pretty sure that even if there was a dying animal right there, he wouldn't be able to do a damn thing about it. Really, the vets were the best to handle that part of things. His job was with the human end.

It didn't escape his notice that the human end of this one was pretty awful. Poisoned animals might not be exactly top priority, but poisoning was definitely a crime, and he'd do what he could. It would be a bit of a change from chasing drug dealers, maybe even a bit of a break.

He made sure he had a pen before he got out of his car and went into the office, his nose wrinkling at the smell of pet food. At least there weren't any more objectionable smells; the place was really clean and tidy.

At the desk, he waited until the girl looked up from her files. "Can I help you?" She smiled at him, eyes checking him out.

Tim didn't roll his eyes; he was in uniform and didn't have an animal with him, so he was pretty sure she knew why he was there. Also, getting checked out by girls wasn't something he really encouraged. He found a smile for her, though, in the name of public relations. "Constable

Geary, here to see Dr. Sauvigon. Is he available?"

"He's just finishing up with a patient. If you want to take a seat, I'll let him know you're here."

There was no one else sitting in the little waiting room. So either the guy didn't book appointments over lunch, or he was a shitty vet.

"If he's going to be a while, I'll have to come back," Tim said, looking around. "But I can sit for a few." He'd give the guy five minutes and then he'd call in, see if there was anything else on the go. He could take this statement any time, really.

She gave him an arch look. "I realize he called you, but without an actual appointment..." She let the sentence trail away and nodded significantly toward the bank of chairs in the waiting room.

He snorted, unable to keep it back. "He called us. I don't need an appointment. I am, however, willing to give him a few minutes to earn his living." But only a few. Tim went to one of the chairs and tried his best not to sprawl. When he sprawled, he tended to hurt himself with his gun belt and all the shit attached to it.

Her look of admiration had turned into a huffy glare, and she got up and headed into the back, her heels clacking.

A few minutes later, a boy with a dog bigger than he was came out of the door beside the reception area, followed by a tall, lanky guy in a lab coat. "Just keep him out of your sister's room, okay, Jason? Barbie dolls are *not* dog food, and one of these days he's going to eat something that'll tear him inside and that would be very bad, okay?"

"Yes, Dr. Ben. It's kind of hard to make him stop, though. He really likes those stupid dolls."

The vet laughed, fluffed the boy's hair, and gave the dog a pat. He watched while the boy led the dog outside, and then turned to Tim. "Constable Geary? Why don't you come back into my office?"

Tim nodded and stood up, one hand holding his pen and the other already reaching for his notebook. "Did that dog really eat a Barbie?" He followed Dr. Sauvigon down a short hall.

The man laughed. "No, he didn't eat *a* Barbie. Today, he was in for Barbie number... I think we're up to five. I shouldn't laugh, though; it would be very serious if he ruptured something."

"Barbies are sharp. I should know." Tim rubbed a spot just behind his left ear. "There was an incident when I was eleven. My sister and In-line Skating Barbie won."

"Well, so far, Jason and his Beastly are far ahead of his sister and her Barbies." Dr. Sauvigon gave him a wink and opened a door, motioning him in to a clean, if somewhat cluttered office.

"Good for them, I guess." Tim went in and looked around curiously before he sat down, once more trying not to sprawl. "Sorry if I rushed you."

"Hmm? Oh, not at all. I was wrapping up the appointment when you came. The sergeant I talked to couldn't give me a specific time you could make it. You're here far sooner than I'd expected, really." Dr. Sauvigon settled in the chair behind the desk covered with neat piles of paper and file folders. "Now, I don't know how much he told you..."

Tim flipped his notebook open. "Poisoned pets, six documented cases so far. Cats and dogs both." He looked up, pen ready. "Do you know if it's the same kind of poison, and is there documentation to support the allegation of poisoning? These animals couldn't have just gotten into garbage or something? Rat poison left in a garage?"

"Six cats and one dog, actually. I have the files on five

of the cats." The vet picked up a file folder and handed it over. "That's for the first five cats. The sixth was this morning and I don't have the tox results back yet. The dog is just a guess on my part. I hadn't connected it until we had a few more cats come in, and she was old for her breed, so I had assumed it was natural causes. All the animals are from the same general area, but far enough from each other that rat poison left in a garage is an awful big stretch."

"But something I'll have to consider." Tim took the folders and started flipping through them. "Um. You're going to have to help me out here, Doc. What am I looking for?" The lab sheets were gibberish to him.

Dr. Sauvigon leaned over the desk and circled an item near the bottom of the sheet. "This is the name of the poison and how much was in the animal's system. It's not the same toxic agent usually found in rat poison, and frankly, the amounts are quite high." Flipping through the sheets, Dr. Sauvigon circled the results for each animal.

Tim caught himself sniffing the air in time to make himself stop. He had no idea what the Doc used on his hair, but damn, he didn't smell like animals at all. He smelled *good*. "So, the amounts indicate deliberate poisoning, in your opinion?" Tim looked down at the chart and tried to figure out what parts per million would be in milligrams. As if he'd know.

"Oh, yes. I suppose it is possible someone's got some poison sitting in their garage, but it would be negligent to have it in an area accessible to the public -- what if a child got into the place? And while one or two animals might do something like that, I can't see six doing it. The odds are very much against it."

Tim nodded and closed the files. "Can I have photocopies of all of these, please? Oh, and is the blood still being stored? It could be evidence, and I'll have to have it taken to our lab for storage."

"Those are photocopies and you may keep them. I sent all the blood I took to the lab." The doc poked through a couple of the piles and then came up with a half dozen cards. He sorted through them and handed one over. "This is the lab's information. I'm not exactly sure how long they store their samples for. I *will* take samples for you on any other cases that come through my office."

"Well, hopefully there won't be many." Tim looked at the card and stuck it in his pocket. "Do the pet owners know that their animals were poisoned? I'll have to talk to them, and I don't want to upset anyone by accident."

"Yes, I've spoken with all of them, though they don't know that I've called in the police."

"That shouldn't be a problem, I wouldn't think." People were usually pretty happy to have things investigated. Well, unless they had something to hide. "Is there anything else I should know, Dr. Sauvigon?"

"Please, call me Ben." He was given a flash of a smile, white teeth gleaming for a moment. "And no, I think it's all there in the file. I appreciate you coming down."

Tim bit back his immediate thought about 'going down' and smiled right back. "It's what I do. Here, take my card. Call me any time, all right? If you think of anything I should know." He took out his own card and wrote his home phone number on the back. "And it's Tim."

Ben took the card, fingers brushing his briefly and, shit, he needed to get laid because that one simple touch went right to his balls.

"Thanks again, Tim." Ben reached for his hand to shake it this time.

Tim held on a bit too long, not able to help himself. Ben had nice hands, soft and warm, but his handshake was anything but weak. "Call me," Tim repeated when he let go. "And I'll let you know if I get anywhere with this."

"I will. Call you, I mean. If something comes up. Regarding the animals." He was given another flash of smile, Ben's cheeks a little flushed.

Oh, right on. Tim grinned at him, reaching for the doorknob. "My home number's on the back. I go off the clock at six this week. Just so you know."

Ben's color got darker, but he nodded. "Good to know."

Still grinning, Tim let himself out and sauntered to the front door. He even gave the girl at the desk a wink, to make up for earlier. Really, if only he didn't have to spend the rest of the afternoon talking to grieving pet owners, his day would just have taken a serious turn for the better.

Chapter Two

Ben sat in his office, staring at the number handwritten on the back of Constable Timothy "call me Tim" Geary's card, debating the pros and cons of giving the guy a call. He wasn't sure if he was trying to talk himself into or out of making the call. On the one hand, it seemed a little ghoulish, making a connection over dead animals. On the other, Harrinton was a small enough town that there weren't a lot of places to go to meet someone gay. Hell, there weren't a lot of places to go to pick anyone up, period.

The rest of his day had gone well and he'd had no more dead pets. He was feeling peckish and didn't really want to go upstairs to his quiet bachelor pad above the practice just yet. A glance at the clock confirmed it was nearly seven p.m. Ben grabbed the phone and dialed the number quickly, before he could change his mind.

It rang twice before Tim picked up, sounding a little out of breath. "Hello?"

"Oh, hi. Sorry, I didn't mean to interrupt anything. I mean. Hi. This is Ben Sauvigon. The vet from this afternoon?" God, he was a dork.

He heard Tim laugh softly, though it didn't sound rude. "You're still there, too. I have Caller ID. And you're not interrupting anything, I was just working out."

Okay, he so didn't need the image of a half-naked, sweaty man doing crunches. Well, he loved the image, but it wasn't doing anything for his composure. "Yeah, I... I haven't eaten yet, I was wondering if you had?"

"Not yet, no." There was a pause and Ben could swear he heard Tim drinking, gulping water or something. "But I'm starving. Do you have anything in mind?"

"I was going to just pick up some Chinese from around the corner. I live above the practice."

"Yeah? Chinese sounds good. I need to shower real fast."

"I could go pick it up and bring it back to my place. You could meet me here?" God, he hoped that didn't sound like he expected anything but dinner to happen. It was just the easiest and he was more comfortable eating at home than in a restaurant.

"That'd be good." Tim sounded pleased, anyway. "I'll be maybe half an hour? Shower and drive. Is the entrance around the side or anything?"

"Yeah, you have to follow the path off the parking lot into the back yard. There anything you don't like?"

"Nosy neighbors. God, did I just say that out loud?"

Ben laughed. "You did. I meant more in the Chinese food line, but I'll remember the other."

"I think I did too many reps on the Bowflex. Um, I like chicken and veggies, sweet and sour more than hot and spicy." Tim was laughing too, sounding a little embarrassed, but not like he was going to bail.

"All right. I'll see you in an hour, then." Ben was chuckling himself as he hung up. He took off his lab coat and hung it over the back of the door, and checked in with Anna, the night nurse. "I'm off for the night. I've got my cell."

"Hopefully it'll be a quiet night." She waved her textbook at him.

"Test tomorrow?"

"Yeah, a big one."

"Good luck." Ben gave her a wave and headed out to pick up food for his date.

His date.

Wow. It had been ages since he'd had one of those.

Maybe his dry spell was over.

Tim was shiny clean and still slightly damp when he got back to the vet clinic. He'd been about right with his time frame guess, but he'd had to sacrifice five minutes of wardrobe planning after his shower, since he'd used the time to jack off instead.

He figured jeans and a long sleeved T-shirt were about the right speed for Chinese take-out.

He parked his car at the end of the little lot, away from the clinic doors. He had no idea if there was anyone still working, but the light was on, and he'd hate to get in the way of a puppy emergency, if such a thing should happen.

The path was right there by his car, and he followed it around to the back, watching the ground for messes; any place that had animals had to have poop, and Tim wasn't going to show up with that on his sneakers, if he could help it. At the top of a flight of stairs, he knocked on the door and waited, looking out at the yard.

A low, heavy bark sounded, and a laugh. "Get out of the way, Tippy, I can't get the door open with you in the way." The door finally opened, Ben looking great in a pair of jeans and a green knit sweater. There was a tan and white basset hound at his feet, long ears all but dragging on the ground. "Hi, Tim."

"Hi." Tim looked down at the pup. "You have a roommate?" He crouched and held out his hand for sniffing.

"Yeah. This is Tippy. She's my best girl. Tippy this is Tim. You be nice to him, okay?"

"Hey, Tippy." Tim let her sniff and lick for a moment, then scratched behind her ears. "How old is she?" He looked way up at Ben from where he was, trying to ignore their position as best he could. He didn't do very well.

Ben's thoughts had to be going in the same direction, because his jeans were starting to get a bulge. Clearing his throat, Ben stepped back, giving him room. "She's eight."

Tim got to his feet and went in, careful not to brush against Ben as he stepped right across Tippy. "She's nice and quiet."

"She's a good old girl." Ben closed the door and led him into the living room. There was a big couch with blue upholstery, a matching easy chair, and a low coffee table covered with Chinese food boxes. The furniture looked well-used, but not shabby. It also looked comfortable.

Tippy climbed up onto the couch, back end scrabbling a little until she hauled it up. Then she sat on the one end, looking like the queen of the couch. Laughing, Ben waved at the couch. "Make yourself comfortable."

Tim nodded and sat at the other end, giving Tippy her space. "Does she like egg rolls?" He reached for one of the containers and peeked inside. "Oh, chicken. Sorry, Tippy. Mine."

Ben laughed. "She's on a special diet, and Chinese food gives her gas. Trust me, you don't want to experience that." Ben sat down between him and Tippy, grabbing another box and opening it up.

"You're probably right." Tim took a moment to think about that and shook his head. "Right, no sharing with the dog. Got it." He leaned back on the couch and started eating. "How was the rest of your day? I kind of wondered, when you called, if you'd gotten another one. Of course, I was hoping an after hours call was about something else entirely."

"No more dead animals, thank God. So it was a pretty good day." Ben smiled, digging into what looked like shrimp and noodles, wielding the chopsticks like an expert. "I was hoping I'd picked up the right signals when you were by."

"Signals?" Tim grinned. "I don't give off signals. I wave flags and use flashing lights. I'm not that good at subtle, and you're a very attractive man."

An attractive man who had a great laugh and a lovely smile. "Well, I'm no expert at flirting, but I do try to notice when a good-looking man thinks it's mutual."

Tim ate more chicken. "I really do like being on the same page." He grinned and nodded to himself. "Makes life a lot easier. And thank you, both for the compliment and this excellent food. It's better than the stuff from Jubilee on King Street."

"Yeah, they know me pretty well there, and Mawmaw Wan always slips in something a little special." Ben reached over and grabbed a little bag. "And the fortune cookies are handmade."

"Seriously?" Tim grinned. "I wonder if they make up the fortunes, too, or if they buy 'em in bulk."

"I think they make them up. Sometimes they're scarily on target." Ben put down the shrimp and opened another box. "Imperial chicken. Spicy, but really good." Ben popped a piece into his mouth and chewed. "So, how long have you been a cop?"

"Since I was twenty. I went to the Police Academy

right out of high school, almost. Did a year in a grocery store first." Tim made a face and reached for another container. "So I'm coming up on ten years. Wow, that's kind of wild." He started in on some chop suey and asked, "And you? How long have you been a vet, how long have you had the clinic, all that stuff."

"I went to the Agriculture College in Guelph right out of high school. Did a couple years internship and then met Stacey, who was looking for a small animals partner to open a clinic in town with. We've been open about three years."

Tim nodded. "Didn't go to the vet college out east? I hear the winters out there are killer." Tim hadn't been anywhere, really. He was a small town kid who loved his small town. "I got hired on by the city mostly so I wouldn't have to go to Regina for the Mounties."
"I got a scholarship for Guelph. It's the best vet program in Canada, really." Ben popped in a couple more bites of chicken before putting the container down. "So, do you like it? Being a cop, I mean."

"Love it." Tim rummaged in his pot for a baby corncob. "I help, I meet people, there's always something new. I don't even mind the endless paperwork, really. And it's a small town, which I think helps in a lot of ways."

"Yeah, I like the small town aspect from the vet angle, as well."

Tim put the carton down, his belly nicely full of good food. It looked like there was enough for a snack later, too. "You get to know your people and their pets, I bet. I mean, it's a long term relationship, right?" He sat back on the couch and noted that Tippy had apparently decided to take a nap.

"Exactly. I get to see the kids grow up, too, you know? I mean it's just been three years, but already some of the kids have gone from pre-teens to teens, really growing up. And you can tell a lot about a person based on how they treat their animals. Hey." He pointed his chopstick at Tim. "You have a pet?"

"I have a stray cat I leave food for, does that count?" He'd had a fish at one point, too, but apparently Bettas didn't live much more than a couple of years. "I grew up with dogs."

"Do you miss having pets?" Ben offered him his choice of fortune cookies.

"Sometimes." Tim took a cookie and held it, turning it over a couple of times. "I work weird hours. It'd be too hard on a dog, I think."

Ben beamed at him and nodded. "Good for you. You don't know how many people we see who don't think it through from the animal's point of view." Tippy was given a pat, her ears flopping around. "This old girl spends most of the day outside in the backyard. Otherwise, she makes the rounds with me if it's winter or nasty weather."

"Plus, you're right there." Tim nodded and broke his cookie open. "Downstairs, here... it's good. Way better than being gone for ten hour shifts and held over a lot of the time."

"Yeah." Ben sat back and smiled. "So, what does your fortune say?"

Tim didn't even glance at the slip of paper. "It says good things come to guys who are smart about pet ownership."

Ben really did have an awesome laugh. "That's cheating." He didn't push Tim to read the actual fortune, though. Instead, Ben opened his own, cheeks heating.

"And what does yours say?" Tim nudged Ben's leg with his own knee, smiling happily. He loved it when guys blushed.

"It says the night begins with a kiss." The words were mumbled, but Tim was pretty sure he'd heard correctly.

"That's a good one." Tim nodded and nudged him again. "And it would be a damn shame to make MawMaw Wan a liar."

"I've got Imperial Chicken breath," Ben warned.

"I don't care." He didn't. He was pretty sure he didn't even care about morning breath.

At his words, Ben leaned in slowly, eyes on his lips.

Tim grinned and leaned too, a bit faster. He hoped to hell that Tippy wasn't the sort to get all protective, because kissing could easily lead to yet more kisses. Maybe even some groping, if he worked it right.

Ben's lips were warm and had a spicy tang to them. When Tim pushed, Ben's lips parted, letting him in. Imperial Chicken was just fine. Tim tasted and licked, deepening the kiss slowly. He still had his fortune cookie in one hand, but with the other he touched Ben's jaw, then his hair, changing the angle just a bit. As kisses went, Tim couldn't find a damn thing wrong with it.

When their lips parted, Ben was smiling at him. "That *was* a good start to the evening."

"If I read my fortune and it says anything at all about backing off, I'm going to ignore it." Tim still had his hand in Ben's hair. "What *do* you use on your hair? You smell fantastic."

"Shampoo. And I was going to suggest a movie." Ben's hazel eyes twinkled.

"Movies are good. I like the shampoo, don't change it." He kissed Tim again before letting him go. "What kind of movie?"

"I've got a pretty eclectic collection. I belong to one of those movie of the month clubs... What do you like?"

"Explosions or foreign art films with subtitles." He figured he could make out through large parts of both kinds and come back knowing exactly as much as he had when he stopped paying attention, and it wouldn't matter.

"Oh, I don't have much in the line of foreign art films, subtitles or no." Ben got up and went over to the bookcase next to a large widescreen TV. He bent down, offering a great view of his jeans-encased ass. "I've got the latest *Die Hard* movie here, though, which I haven't seen yet. Have you?"

"Nope." Tim shook his head and watched Ben's ass. He kind of hoped he could say the same thing by the end of the night.

"Cool!" Ben got the movie into the DVD player and tossed him the remote. "I'm just going to get the leftovers cleared up. Oh, I should warn you -- if the movie's too loud, Tippy'll howl at it, so don't pump the volume too much."

"Got it." He could have quiet explosions. He got them past the piracy warnings while Ben put the food away, then leaned over to Tippy. He checked to make sure Ben was still out of the room and whispered, "If you give us the whole couch, I promise to bring you designer dog treats from the shop downtown."

The big brown eyes stared at him, Tippy not moving an inch. It was clearly *her* corner.

"Help me out, here. Ham-flavored chew strips. You know him. You love him. I get it. But I'm a nice guy, I swear." He tried to look utterly trustworthy.

Tippy woofed in her deep hound voice and settled in more firmly, head on the arm of couch.

"You want something to drink?" Ben called from the kitchen. "I've got beer, water, tea, coffee or juice. Sorry, no soft drinks -- they're the devil's work."

"Pop is out, but beer is in?" Ben really was his kind of guy. "I'll take one, thanks. Tippy seems fond of her part of the couch."

Ben came back with a couple of bottles of the local

brew, caps already off. "Oh yeah, she deigns to let others sit, though I've known her to chase some people right off. My mother even thinks of sitting on the couch and Tippy gets all bitchy."

"So, I'm not doing so bad, then?" He reached for one of the bottles and grinned. "What do you do when you want to stretch out, though?"

Ben sat fairly close, giving Tippy her room. So there was one advantage to her being on the couch. "She makes an excellent footrest."

"Works for me." Tim slipped an arm around Ben and hit play on the remote. "Let's see what Bruce Willis is bringing to the party this time."

"My bet is on lots of explosions, swearing, and an awesome bod for a guy as old as he is." Ben settled in, seemingly just fine with Tim's arm where it was.

Chapter Three

Ben fell asleep partway through the movie. It wasn't a comment on the movie itself, or the company, but on the fact that he'd been down at the clinic twice the night before for emergencies and was really tired.

He woke with a start during the climax of the movie, face plastered against Tim's shoulder, drooling for Pete's sake. "Oh, man." He sat up, blinking, trying to surreptitiously wipe the drool off the side of his mouth. "Shit. Sorry."

"It's okay." Tim's voice was quiet and kind of amused. "I like to think of it as meaning you're really, really comfortable with me. But I'm pretty sure it means you're really, really tired, so I should take off."

"Yeah, we had a couple of emergency calls last night." Ben shook his head, slowly waking up. He checked the clock. It was only ten-thirty. "We could go do dessert at the ice cream place over on Maple. They make their own ice cream." Dessert was the least he owed Tim, after falling asleep on him.

"Yeah?" Tim stretched, his legs and arms going stiff and straight for a moment. "You're sure?"

"Yeah, I'll be awake for hours now after napping." He found himself staring and he licked his lips before continuing. "If you want to." For all he knew, he'd totally blown it with the guy; he wouldn't blame Tim if that was true.

"I can pretty much always go for ice cream." Tim finished his stretch and sat up straight. "Chocolate mint."

"I like soft-serve vanilla the best. Dipped in chocolate *and* nuts." He grinned, pleased he hadn't totally turned Tim off. He gave Tippy a good petting. "Be good while we're gone, sweetie."

"I don't think she's moved since I got here." Tim stood up and held out his hand. "It's a nice night. We're close enough to walk?"

"Yeah, sure. And she's an old girl, she's not nearly as active as she used to be." He laughed. "Not that hounds are the most active dogs in the world to start with."

"She's not exactly a lab, that's for sure. Still, she's pretty cute."

"Hey. Do not insult a man's dog. She's a sweetheart and a better friend than a lot of people I know." He glared at Tim, but found he couldn't keep it up. "Come on, let's go before she decides to gnaw off your foot."

"Oh, yes, she's a ferocious beast." Tim was teasing, grinning at him. "I'm in great danger. You must help me!"

"Get off the couch and I'll buy you an ice cream cone, you goof." Laughing, Ben held out his hand and hauled Tim to his feet.

"Oh, dinner, a movie, *and* dessert. You really do know how to win a guy." Tim held on tight to his hand. "I might even kiss you goodnight."

"I was kind of hoping you would."

"I'd like to kiss you now."

"Yeah? Okay." He'd liked the kiss they'd shared. It has been slow and good. Full of potential. He was a couple inches taller than Tim, and had to lean down just a little to bring their mouths together.

Tim leaned in close, though, not shy about moving into Ben's space as they kissed. He had a hand on Ben's shoulder and the other one on Ben's hip, just as easy as anything. He was warm and strong, and kissed like he meant it.

Ben groaned. It would be so easy to get lost in the kisses, to let them lead to more. He wanted more than a one-night thing, though. He wanted to get to know Tim a little first, so he stepped away, breathing a little heavy.

Tim's eyes were huge and dark and he was breathing a bit faster, too. "So. Ice cream?"

Ben nodded and led the way, locking the door behind them. He patted his front jeans pocket, double-checking that he had the emergency phone on him.

"It's all there. Trust me."

He shot Tim a look. "What?"

Tim just grinned and gave him a long look up and down. "Just... everything. It's all where it's supposed to be."

"Oh." Ben could feel his cheeks heating up. "I was just making sure I had the clinic phone. In case there was an emergency." He ducked his head and high-tailed it down the stairs.

"You're very cute when you blush," Tim informed him as he caught up. "I'll lay off, though."

"Well, I like that you like what you see." He slowed to a stroll, the evening air cooling down his cheeks.

"I really like what I see." Tim's voice was emphatic and a bit husky. "But I'll try to pull back on the baser urges. For a while, anyway."

"I just don't want to rush into anything. I'd rather

spend some time." He knew it was corny and old-fashioned, but it was a part of who he was. And one of the reasons why he hadn't been laid in a long while.

"I got time," Tim said easily, casually. His hand brushed Ben's, their fingers tangling briefly. "As long as you can put up with horrible and unpredictable hours, anyway. Oh, and a rather stressful job. And some bad habits. I'm going to stop talking now."

Ben nudged their hips as they walked. "Well, let's see, maybe I can put up with that if you can put up with emergency calls in the middle of the night, fingernail biting, and my partner."

"Now, why do I think you're not referring to Tippy?" Tim gave him a long look. "The vet you met at school, right?"

"Yeah. Her name is Stacey. She's... a great lady, really she is. But she takes getting used to." He loved her like the sister he'd never had. "Oh, and then there's my mother... maybe we should focus on *your* bad habits."

"Uh, I work out all the time, I eat bad food -- which means I work out more -- and I hog the shower. I've been told I snore, but I'm sure that's not true. I'm kind of a slob."

"Hmm... I don't know, Tim." Ben eyed the muscles he could see beneath Tim's shirt. The very nice muscles that made his cock happy. "That working out thing? It might be a deal breaker."

Tim grinned at him and flexed a tiny bit. "You'll get bored watching, maybe."

"Maybe." But he'd bet he wouldn't get tired of touching. He shoved his hands into his pockets and nodded toward the ice cream shop as they turned the corner. "That's it just ahead."

"This is going to mean extra crunches, I can tell from here. They have waffle cones, don't they?" Tim was sniffing the air happily. "Yum."

"They do. And all sorts of sprinkles and shit. And, like I said, the ice cream is homemade, all of it made with whole milk and cream and stuff. So it tastes amazing." He grinned. "The way to a man's heart, eh?"

"This man, anyway." Tim was actually speeding up, following the scent. "Why didn't I know this place was here?"

"Yeah, I'm surprised. I thought cops knew all the good places in town." He held the door open for Tim. It was pretty crowded, as usual, though not as bad as he'd sometimes seen it.

"That's doughnuts. This is ice cream." Tim looked around and sniffed again. "I think I'll just move in here."

Ben laughed, delighted with Tim's outright enjoyment of the smells. "Wait until you *taste* it."

Tim went right up to the counter and read the menu avidly, double-checking on a couple of flavors. "I'll take a scoop of chocolate mint and one of double chocolate fudge, in a bowl, with cherries," he told the girl. He flashed Ben a huge smile and shrugged. "I can work out extra tomorrow."

Laughing, Ben ordered strawberry in a plain cone, no cherries. They grabbed their orders and went to sit at one of the little tables out on the back deck. His ice cream was good, the strawberry flavor strong and the ice cream full of big chunks of actual berries.

"This town is not big," Tim said between one bite and the next. He was using his spoon to gesture while he talked, waving it like a baton to indicate the area around them. "Why didn't I know there was homemade ice cream? That's just not fair. Make me feel better and tell me it's because I grew up on the other side of town, or the shop is new this year, or something."

Ben couldn't resist teasing. "You want me to lie to you? On our first date? Isn't that a bad way to start a relationship?"

"At this stage, I think a little white lie is okay. As long as it's not about something important, however." Tim winked at him and filled his mouth with more ice cream.

"Then, yeah, it's only been open for a little while. Just ignore the date on the front window." God, Ben hadn't had this much fun flirting in a long time. And Tim made it easy to do.

"Cool." Tim licked his spoon and looked pleased as hell. "It's really good. If we spend a lot of time together, though, we're going to have to make this place for treats only -- I can't work out *that* much."

Ben laughed, but at the same time, he started to wonder if it was going to bother Tim that he didn't work out, and that he wasn't overly concerned if he didn't have six-pack abs. Oh, he appreciated them on others, and Tim's muscles were a definite turn-on, which just made him wonder all that much more.

Tim finished up his ice cream and sat back with a happy sigh. "That was amazing." His foot was somehow right next to Ben's, rubbing a little.

"Thank you." He rubbed right back.

"So, do you have an early morning tomorrow?"

"Yeah, I start at eight. The biggest thing is the emergency calls the last two nights, though. They each took a whack of sleep time with them." The nap had helped, but Ben knew he shouldn't get to bed too late. "Maybe we can do this again sometime."

"I'd like that." Tim nodded and rubbed at his foot again before standing up. "I'll stop by the clinic, too. Hopefully with an update for you, and maybe lunch."

"If you're going to bring lunch, you should call first and make sure I'm able to take a break. Some days we get emergencies in or I get behind." He didn't want Tim to think he wasn't interested. "I'll tell Amy -- she's my receptionist -- to let you know if you call and ask how my schedule is looking."

Tim grinned. "I don't think Amy likes me. I pulled rank on her today and she stopped checking me out."

"Oh, you've put your foot in it there -- she likes to think she's the queen bee." Still, if he told her she needed to put Tim through or give him information, she would. He did still pay her salary, after all.

Tim didn't seem terribly bothered. "I figured I was better off with you checking me out, anyway." He winked again and held out his hand. "Walk me to my car?"

Ben grabbed the offered hand and bumped their hips together. "Seeing as it's parked at my place, it would be kind of rude if I didn't."

"That's what I thought." Tim laughed and threaded their fingers together. "So. Dinner, a movie, a nap, and ice cream. I think this was a pretty successful first date."

"Oh, good. I do, too." He'd been worried Tim would be pissed they hadn't gotten together in the bedroom. A lot of guys expected it to be a part of a first date.

"Maybe next time I can come up with a movie that'll keep you awake." Tim was teasing, his eyes sparkling as they walked under a street light.

"I don't know, if explosions and swearing don't do it..."

"Maybe something with subtitles will -- you'll need to keep your eyes open."

"There you go." He squeezed Tim's hand, enjoying their easy banter.

Tim squeezed back, rubbing the back of his hand. "I'll see if I can find one that's not terrible," he said with a laugh. "Oh, and does Tippy let you out to date, or does she like to keep an eye on everything?"

"Oh, she's a sweetheart and never complains if I leave her alone for a couple of hours." More than that and she got vocal, though.

Tim nodded. "So, short dates away, longer dates at your place. Got it."

"I can always get a dogsitter." He didn't like doing it a lot, but Tippy was happy enough occasionally spending time with whoever manned the desk overnight.

"I just like to have all the options and rules set out." Tim laughed sheepishly. "I think it's partly the cop in me. Plus, I just like to know where I stand. I didn't mean to sound like I was planning out the next month of your life."

"It's okay. It's nice knowing you're interested enough to ask the questions."

They turned into the clinic's parking lot. Tim's car was the only one there.

"Quiet night." Tim looked around as they walked over to his car. "You've got good lighting here. I'm sure it helps for those late night emergencies. Not so great for making out next to my car, though."

Ben laughed. "You really are a cop at heart, aren't you?" Then he leaned in and pressed their lips together, not caring if someone noticed them just kissing.

To Tim's credit, he didn't waste time laughing or teasing or even ducking for cover. Instead, he slipped one hand around Ben's waist and tugged him a little bit closer, returning the kiss with a sweet and soft one of his own.

Their lips clung as the kiss ended and Ben sighed, taking a step back. "We definitely have to do that again."

"The kissing or the date? Because I completely agree." Tim smiled at him and got his car keys out of his pocket. "Really."

"Well, both, I guess." Ben chuckled and took another step back, shoving his hands in his pockets for something to do with them.

"Good." Tim opened his car door and climbed in. "I'll call you tomorrow about the pets. And very soon about a second date. Thanks, Ben. I had a great time."

"Me, too. Talk to you later." He waved.

Tim closed his door and started the car, then pulled out a moment later. He lifted his hand in a wave and drove away, heading away from the ice cream shop. But Ben was pretty sure he'd back for more than ice cream soon.

He was whistling as he made his way to the back.

Chapter Four

Tim wondered if he was pushing his luck.

He hadn't precisely rushed right over to the clinic as soon as his shift started, but it kind of felt a bit lame, anyway, how fast he'd headed that way. He'd put in a few hours on assorted cases, talked to a lot of people, and even filed some paperwork. But as soon as he had a free moment, there he was, pulling into the lot and hoping Ben was there. It was too late for lunch, but he'd brought a treat anyway.

The parking lot wasn't empty this time. There were a couple of cars and a truck, and when Tim pushed the door open, he was neatly pounced upon by an itty-bitty puppy, all mouth and tail.

"Oh, hey there," he said, bending down to let the little thing sniff and lick. "No, no. Not that, buddy." He held his paper bag high as the puppy's owner tried to pick it up or at least drag it off Tim's ankle.

Tim didn't wince when the puppy's teeth dug in. He was a cop. He could deal with playing dogs.

"Sorry!" The owner, a teenage boy with long hair and a high blush, said. "She's a little... energetic."

"Not a problem." Tim smiled at the kid and went up to the desk, wondering if he could charm his way back into Amy's good graces. "Hi, there."

"You again." She glanced down at her book. "I don't see an appointment for you..."

Well, that killed that hope. Tim sighed and shrugged. "Active investigation. I don't need an appointment. Is he in?"

"Of course he's in -- the question is whether we can fit you in. What was your name again?"

Tim leaned forward. In his calmest, most controlled cop voice he said, "My name is Constable Timothy Geary, and no, it is not a question of if you can fit me in. This is a police matter, and I take precedence. I *will* see him before other clients if it is regarding the investigation. If it's a personal matter, of course, I'll wait. Are we clear?"

She pursed her lips. "As it happens, I have a note here to show you to his office if you come in. All I needed was your name."

"He knows my name, and I gave it to you yesterday. Are we going to have a problem?"

"Of course not. And we have a lot of people come through here, you know, I can't be expected to remember everyone's name." She stood and pointed to the door. "If you go through there, I'll show you where his office is."

"I know the way, thanks. I was in it yesterday." Yeah, she hated him. He hoped she got over it soon, because he wasn't terribly fond of her either. "I won't keep him long." He went through the door and turned down the short hall, heading to Ben's office and hoping he was alone.

The office door was ajar and the office was empty. No Ben.

"Great." No way was dear Amy going to help him out and tell Ben he was there, either. He'd lay money on it. With a sigh, Tim put the paper bag on Ben's desk and sat down. Maybe he could do some actual work while he waited. Or maybe he could doodle on his notepad. He definitely wasn't going back to Amy to find out where Ben was.

It was about ten minutes before Ben came in, eyes widening in surprise. "Tim!"

"Amy hates me."

Ben blinked, dropping a file on his desk. "What did you do to her?"

Tim grinned and nodded. "Nice. How about what she did to me?"

"Okay, what did she do to you?" Instead of going around, Ben leaned his ass against the front of the desk.

"She pulled rank, said she didn't remember my name, tried to tell me that she'd 'fit me in' to your schedule, wanted to show me to your office -- like I don't know where it is -- and then didn't tell you I was here." Tim grinned wider. "She thinks she's alpha, but I've got bigger boots. You're hot. Kiss me?"

Chuckling, Ben bent and brushed their lips together. "She's alpha of that desk, but the real alpha around here is Stacey."

"I'll remember to wear my gun so I don't feel threatened." Tim smiled and leaned in for another kiss before letting Ben get away. "I brought you a mid-afternoon snack."

Ben glanced at his watch and then smiled. "All right. I can take a break. Are you the snack?"

Tim felt his eyebrows shoot up. "I am now." Hell, yes. If that door locked he'd happily let Ben do whatever he wanted.

Laughing, Ben looked around, finding the paper bag on the desk. "What's in the bag?"

Damn. "A taste of the best bakery a cop can find in this

town." Tim nodded toward it. "Danish, not a doughnut, but good like you won't believe."

"What flavor?" Ben asked, opening the bag and peeking in.

"Cherry. It was all they had, but I swear it's the best one. Real cherries, handmade pastry..." If a way to a man's heart and into his pants was through sweets, Tim had all his money on McCaully's Bakery.

"It smells good. There's only one in here, though -- did you already eat yours?"

Tim laughed. "Remember that ice cream last night? Forty-five minutes on the machines or an hour running tonight. I'd rather spend that hour with you."

"You're a little obsessed about the working out thing." Ben took a bite of the Danish and made happy noises, nodding. "Yeah, this is good."

"I'm a little obsessed with not failing the physicals and with being on the relay team next month." Tim had made the team last year, but hadn't trained well enough; he'd thought he was going to fall apart before he crossed the finish line. "But I'll always make time for ice cream."

"Relay team?" Ben broke off a small bite and offered it over.

Tim took it, unable to resist. He even used his fingers rather than his mouth, which he thought made him a very good boy, indeed. "The annual charity fundraiser? Us versus the fire department. Huge amount of rivalry, lot of money raised. But I'm up for SWAT next year, so it's more about pride, this time. And kicking the FD's ass, of course."

"That sounds like an afternoon of eye candy. Why have I never been before?"

"I have no idea." Tim grinned at him and ate the bite of Danish happily. "Come watch this year. Cheer me on. It's a two day event, though, so everyone in both departments can do it and still work their shifts."

"Two days of hot, fit men sweating it up? You don't have to talk me into it." Ben finished off his Danish, licking his lips clean.

Tim watched his mouth and shifted in the chair, his belt creaking. "Yeah, it's a nice weekend. But that's why I'm so full on the working out right now; I kind of have to prove myself, this time around."

Ben was checking him out. "Well, you're looking good, if there was any doubt."

"You think?" Tim preened and looked down at himself. "Kind of hard to tell with all this gear on." He looked up at Ben through his lashes and gave him a smile. "You're welcome to look all you want and check to make sure, too. Although, maybe not right now, with Amy mere feet away."

Laughing, Ben folded up the bag and tossed it at the garbage can. "I'd love to check it out. But I have patients waiting..."

"And I have to actually talk to you so I don't feel guilty about pulling rank on Amy." Tim rolled his eyes and flipped open his notebook. "I talked to all but one of the owners -- Cosmo's family is out of town -- and I've done a walk-through of the neighborhood. Our lab is going to contact yours about taking custody of the blood samples for chain of evidence. What I need to know now is, generally, how long after the animals ingest the poison would they appear sick enough for the owners to bring them in? Do you know?"

"Within twenty-four hours."

"Can you narrow it down any more? Or give me a list of when they were brought in? Were they all emergency visits, or were there appointments?" Tim smiled and shook his head. "Sorry, I tend to ask too many questions at once. I'm trying to see if they were poisoned at about the same time of day, or if there's no pattern at all."

"I'll have to check the files." Ben went behind his desk and started sorting through files.

"I can go back and talk to the owners more if I need to. So far it looks like some were sicker than others -- the ones whose owners were out during the day and didn't find their pets until after work or school. Makes it hard, when the victims can't talk."

"Tell me about it." Ben pulled out a few files and nodded. "Here we go. The sicker ones were here in the evening on emergency calls. Two who weren't as sick came in during the day. So I think it's happening overnight."

"Do you think..." Tim frowned and looked at his notes. "Do you think, in your medical opinion, that the doses are determined by the size of the animal? Were the smaller ones really sick? Or were all the pets about the same size?"

"They were mostly the same size. And I think I know where you're going with this, but I can't tell you if size-specific doses were used or if something was left out and they ate it at random." Ben frowned, looked at the files again and shook his head. "No, I can't determine that at all. And even if it was something left out at random, one animal's possibly going to eat more than another."

Tim nodded. "Right, of course. Okay. I'll add everything to the file and do some brainstorming. Right now I'm going to head to our lab and see if the paperwork is done up for the blood." He stood up and looked at Ben. "Is it too soon to see about a second date? I'm not really good at playing hard to get."

"It's only too soon if tonight is too soon to actually have the date." Ben's eyes shone happily.

"Not by my standards. Dinner again? Or maybe a walk through the park?" Tim was pretty sure he was grinning like a dork.

"How about we combine them and have a picnic?"

Oh, that sounded great. Grass and food and stars and blankets. "Perfect. I'll pick you up. What time are you done for the day today?" Tim was already planning the food. He had some awesome chicken from the deli.

"Five-thirty today, but I usually take about a half hour to do paperwork and check up on tomorrow's patients. I'll need longer if I'm doing the food."

Tim shook his head. "I've got the food this time. I don't go off shift until six, though, and I'll need to get it together and shower. Say about seven?"

"Seven sounds perfect. That'll give me some quality time with Tippy before we meet up. Dorchester Park?"

"If you'd like. I can pick you up, if you'd prefer." Tim tucked his notebook away and got ready to leave, his day suddenly brighter.

"I kind of like the idea of being picked up." Ben grinned, standing and coming around the desk to meet him.

"Oh, good. Because I'm kinda thinking you have been." Tim checked to make sure no one was coming down the hall and reached for Ben, wanting another kiss before he left.

Ben's lips met his eagerly, though the kiss stayed soft and easy. He tasted like the cherry Danish. Tim licked at the corners of Ben's mouth, chasing the flavor, wanting to sink right into the kiss and enjoy the sweetness for as long as possible.

Ben backed away far too soon. "I'm sorry, Tim. I have to get back to my patients."

Tim nodded and took a shuddering breath. "Yeah. Okay. Best not get too carried away." He shook his head and grinned at the floor. "Not here, anyway. I'll see you tonight." He stepped into the hall and tried not to look too smug.

Ben's laughter followed him.

Tim gave up on not looking smug and sauntered past Amy's desk. "See you tomorrow, Amy. Have a good day."

Her mouth dropped open, and then snapped shut. She very firmly turned and gave the lady at the desk a brilliant smile. "How can I help you?"

Still grinning, Tim headed out and got in his car. Okay. Picnic in the park. He could totally do that. A few more hours of work, then it would be time to prove he could plan a decent date and carry on a conversation that was about more than sweet food and working it off.

Composing a shopping list in his head, he headed back to the station to write up his notes in some kind of actual order and then chase down the lab work. He hoped he had a clean shirt.

Chapter Five

Picking an outfit for a walk in the park and a picnic should have been easy, but Ben found himself standing barefoot and topless, jeans zipped up but not buttoned as he looked through the shirts in his closet and the T-shirts in his dresser.

This was stupid; Tim wasn't going to care if he threw on the first thing he grabbed.

There was a knock at the door, a confident rap of knuckles on the window that could only mean his date was there.

Damn.

He grabbed a light gray T-shirt and tugged it on, heading for the door to let Tim in as Tippy gave her low, warning bark.

"Hey." Tim was leaning on the outside frame of the door, a dog cookie in his hand. "I brought Her Highness a bribe. It's from that place downtown, next to the butcher... you know the one. Overpriced pet stuff and homemade biscuits for beloved doggies."

Ben laughed. "I know the one."

Tim bent down and held the treat out to Tippy. "This

is for you, princess. I'm going to take the handsome prince out for a bit, treat him good. Okay? I promise to have him home at a reasonable hour. Mostly."

Ben chuckled and gave Tippy a pet. "I have to find socks."

"I like the bare feet." Tim was looking at his toes and grinning. "I like it all, actually."

Tim was dressed casually as well, in black jeans, sneakers, and a blue T-shirt that really showed off his muscles.

Ben had to curl his fingers into his palms to keep from reaching out. "Well, if we're going out, I've got to put on socks and shoes."

He got a fast once over, from his toes to his hair and back down again. "Are we in a rush?"

Ben rested his weight on one leg. "What have you got in mind?"

"Mauling. But I'm trying to be really good, so maybe half a mauling."

"If there's mauling, there probably won't be walking in the park."

Tim actually looked torn, looking away and down the stairs and then back to smile at Ben. "Get your socks and shoes. Maybe the park will be really dark."

"Or we can come back here." He leaned in and took a quick kiss before heading back to the bedroom to grab a clean pair of socks and his sneakers.

He could hear Tim's voice, apparently directed to Tippy. "I think he likes me. And you better not be one for hogging *all* the flat surfaces."

Tippy's low woof answered Tim and Ben grinned, grabbing a sweater, too, before heading back into the living room.

"Ready? I hope you like chicken and assorted cheeses. I should have asked this afternoon, but I knew I had stuff at home. Fresh berries, some great rolls..." Tim stopped talking and laughed. "I haven't eaten yet, can you tell?"

"Considering you wanted to stop for mauling first? No, I can't." He gave Tim a wink and grabbed his keys. "Okay, Tippy, you be good. I won't be too long, I promise."

"I was thinking we could start at the north end," Tim said as he led the way down the stairs and around to his car. "And maybe find a nice place to eat over by the pond? We should be able to see the stars from there if we stay for a couple of hours."

"Sure. Why don't we aim for the pond, but kind of otherwise leave our plans more open?" Ben liked not being planned to death.

"Sure, that sounds good to me. I'm kind of hoping that there's a soccer game or something going that we can watch. Or maybe the ducks will be really cute."

"I thought you wanted to find a bush to neck behind or something." He locked the door and they headed down the stairs.

"That, too. And I know the good ones." Tim laughed and walked to the car. "I could tell you stories about the people I've rousted in that park."

Ben shot Tim a look. "Are you serious?" There went any chance of them necking in the park. He'd wait until they were back home, thank you very much.

"Mostly high school kids." Tim grinned. "But I do know the good bushes. Come on, let's go."

He snorted and climbed in, pulling on his belt. "No bushes."

"Back seat, then?"

"What's wrong with the bed?"

Tim gave him a fast look. "Not a damn thing. But if we don't change the subject, this is going to be the fastest walk in the park in the history of second dates."

"You're a hornball," he accused, trying hard not to laugh.

"I confess." Tim gave him a hangdog look and drove toward the park. "I admit it. I like sex. I like you. I think mixing the two would be a pretty fantastic thing."

Ben's chuckles turned into outright laughter. "I think so, too. Just not in public."

"Public would be bad." Tim nodded at him and reached over to take his hand. "But that's not to say I won't be thinking about it, anyway."

"They say anticipation makes things better."

"Why do you think I opted for the park and not going right in? It was only partially about the food." Tim squeezed his hand and gave him a look that was almost a leer. "Now, stop distracting me with the hotness of you and I'll get us to where we're going."

"Okay... I'll think ugly thoughts?"

Tim laughed and turned a corner. "You do that. I'll just drive."

"You know it's not as easy as it looks -- thinking ugly. We're kind of programmed against that sort of thing." He liked the way Tim drove. It was confident without being cocky. And the man's thigh muscles shifted and flexed beneath his jeans.

"Oh, yes. The manly programming of being as hot as possible to capture the attentions of the very best mates." Tim nodded wisely. "Also, if you're trying, it's not working. You're still hot."

"Yeah, well, I'm not the hottest guy in the car. Not by a long shot."

"Stop." Tim grinned at him and winked. "You'll make me blush." He might not have been blushing, exactly, but he did look faintly embarrassed by the compliment, and flattered.

"It's just true." He took a good look, enjoying the

way that T-shirt outlined Tim's muscles. He might have teased Tim about being obsessed with working out, but, boy, had it paid off. In spades. He sat on his fingers to keep from reaching out and stroking anything.

"When we get there," Tim said slowly, looking dead ahead, "there's going to be a little bit of kissing in the car. Just a little."

"You think we can keep it to a little bit?" He wasn't sure he was going to be able to keep his hands to himself, once he started touching.

"Of course. I have amazing self-control." Tim's lips twitched as he said it.

"But I don't." As if to prove it, he yanked his left hand out from under his thigh and reached over to touch Tim's thigh.

"That could be a problem, then." Tim glanced down, but made no attempt to move the hand. Instead, he turned into the park's little collection of parking spaces and flexed his thigh.

Ben felt his cheeks heat as that little flex made his cock go sproing. He bit his bottom lip and squeezed.

Tim hissed through his teeth and pulled the car into a spot, slamming it into park with a bit more than the necessary force. He turned the key and the engine died, then Tim shifted in his seat. "A little kissing," he said firmly.

Ben glanced around. It was still light out, and they weren't the only car in the lot. "Tim..." He really didn't want to get caught necking in Tim's car by anyone.

"Yes? Daylight and public spots help my self-control. I promise not to maul."

"Just one kiss." He leaned toward Tim, his seatbelt pulling him up short.

Laughing softly, Tim leaned in and kissed him, just the once. A brush of his mouth, a lick from his tongue, and a hand petting along the top of Ben's thigh. "There. That'll do for a while. Maybe. Can you carry the blanket? I'll get the food."

"Yeah, I can do the blanket." His voice was a little thick.

"Don't do the blanket. Do me. Later." Tim kissed him again, really fast, and got out of the car. "Or, you know. The other way."

Ben managed to get his seatbelt finally undone and climbed out, grabbing the blanket from the back seat. "We'll see what comes up," he suggested.

"It's already up. Yours, too." Tim beamed at him and passed him the blanket, then picked up the large wicker basket. "I hope water is okay to drink -- I didn't think to buy wine."

"You're driving so that's probably best. It might be awkward if you had to arrest yourself." He fell easily into step with Tim, walking along one of the paths.

"You know, that thought occurred to me while we were talking about bushes." Tim took his hand. "Is this okay?"

"This is just fine. It's making out in public that I'm leery of." He squeezed Tim's hand as they wandered.

Tim shot him a glance. "Have you been threatened?"

"What?"

"I'm a cop. Have you been threatened or harassed because you're gay?"

"Oh!" Ben shook his head. "Sorry, I didn't make the connection. No, nothing like that. I just... I think it's a private thing, you know? I don't want to see a pair of teenagers making out in front of me, and I don't want to put on a show, either."

Tim nodded and relaxed a bit. "Okay, that's cool." He hitched the basket up a bit higher as they walked around a tree stump. "I don't mind private."

"Thanks for worrying, though."

Tim chuckled. "That was only partly cop. I'm gay, too -- hate to break it to you if you hadn't figured that out -- and I tend to leap to conclusions sometimes."

Ben gasped. "You're gay, too?"

"I know, I know. I hide it well."

"You do. I'd never have guessed. Well, except for the part where you came on to me."

Tim laughed. "That part's usually the dead giveaway. Mind you, you asked me out first. Maybe I just misunderstood your intentions or something."

"And the kissing? Was that a misunderstanding, too?"

"No, that was me trying to get in your pants. How am I doing so far?"

"Well, five minutes ago I would have said you were a sure thing, but if you're not actually gay..."

"Hey, I'm totally gay." Tim looked around. "I'm walking through a park, holding a picnic basket with one hand and you with the other. It doesn't get much gayer without ruby slippers."

"You have ruby slippers? This, I have to see. Do you have a blue and white gingham-checked dress to go with them?" He was going to bust a gut any minute now, from keeping his laughter inside.

Tim gave him a long look, his eyes twinkling and his lips twitching. "The only way you'll ever see me in a dress is if it's Halloween. Then, all bets are off."

"Oh, we are so dressing up for Halloween this year." His laughter died as he realized he'd committed the faux pas of assuming they'd still be together in six months. And on the second date, at that.

"You can be Toto. Or maybe the Tin Man." Tim tugged his hand, and they moved deep into the wooded path that led to the pond. "You sure about that bushes thing?"

"Yeah, I'm sure. Besides, I'm too old to be rolling around on the ground, having twigs poking in uncomfortable spots."

"Too old?" Tim shook his head. "Not by half. However, we should keep the blanket all neat for eating on. Oh, look. Lots of places to spread out."

"Not too close to the ducks -- they'll rush us if they think they can take us, and then eat all our food."

"Good point. And I have no authority with them, at all." Tim led them over toward a bit of trees, well away from the ducks. "Here?"

"This'll do fine." Ben spread out the blanket and laughed as his stomach growled loudly. "You'd better have lots of food in that basket."

"I have a vast amount of food, I promise." Tim knelt down next to him and started to unpack. Aside from plates and paper napkins, there was chicken, ham, and turkey, all deli-sliced and packed into a container. Mustard, mayo, bread, grapes, three kinds of cheese, two peaches, some strawberries and a dish of raspberries appeared, and then bottles of water. "Ta-da!"

"Wow. That's quite the selection." Ben was impressed. He sat cross-legged on the blanket and grabbed a few grapes, popping them into his mouth one at a time.

"I was hungry when I was packing it all up." Tim laughed and sprawled next to him, then reached for the bread. "I love sandwiches. A lot."

"Is there butter?" he asked. "What if I want ketchup, or pickles?"

"Then you'll need to find another gay cop to cater to your whims." Tim grinned at him and stole a grape.

He laughed and stole a piece of bread in return. "Gimme some ham and cheese, man."

Tim passed them over, and the next few minutes were

spent building sandwiches and arguing over which kind of cheese was better with ham -- Swiss, or anything other than Swiss. Tim finally gave up and just gave Ben all the cheese so he could do what he wanted, and the two of them sat back to eat, smiling happily.

They may have looked a little ridiculous, but neither of them seemed to care.

They washed the sandwiches down with the water and then spent a few minutes eating the fruit. The peaches weren't really ripe, but that meant there weren't any juices running down his chin, and the strawberries and raspberries more than made up for them.

"So, feeling less hungry and likely to chase the ducks?" Tim tossed his peach pit into the plastic bag they were using for refuse.

"I'm good." Ben lay back, looking up into the leaves of the tree, enjoying the company, the feeling of being full and happy.

"You are." Tim said it softly and stretched out next to him, lying on his side. "Funny, smart, and still really hot. You're good."

He turned his head to smile at Tim. "You're pretty good for my ego, man."

"But I'm not just blowing smoke." Tim gave him another one of those long looks, like he was drinking him in. "I'm serious."

Ben's cock got a little bit happy at that look and he shifted to his side, too, so he wasn't lying there with an obvious hard-on for anyone who happened to walk by to see.

"Tell me..." Tim looked thoughtful for a moment. "You went to Westlake High, right? I was at Brookside, and we were in different years. So I can't make small talk by gossiping about people we knew way back when." Tim grinned suddenly. "So, you have to put up with me relentlessly hitting on you, I guess."

"You could tell me about your day." Not that he didn't enjoy Tim hitting on him, but he was genuinely interested in Tim.

"Pretty much the usual. I worked five or six cases at the same time, fitting in interviews and checking notes, entering anything tangible into the system computers. I've got a couple of theft cases going on, I'm prepping for court on an old assault, and then I spent most of the afternoon getting your blood evidence safely into our lab and talking to pet owners." He shrugged one shoulder. "Kind of typical. Usually there's more paperwork, though."

"I've got to admit, that doesn't sound nearly as exciting as I'd pictured."

"I know, right? It's a bit of a letdown. I don't even ever use my gun except for routine cleaning and keeping up my proficiency scores at the range. I do chase people once in a while, though. That's more a pain in the ass than exciting, though."

Ben bit his lip, but he couldn't contain his laughter at Tim's last comment.

"You have the sense of humor of a twelve-year-old." Tim beamed at him. "I like it."

"What's your sense of humor like?" These things were important.

"Fifteen, at least. I hardly ever find fart jokes funny anymore." Tim was laughing too, his face bright with it in the last rays of the sunset.

"Well, that's because you don't work with kids all day. Let me tell you, fart jokes are supreme for many a pet owner who comes through my office!" He couldn't help himself from reaching out to touch Tim's face, fingertips moving gently on Tim's skin.

"I bet the kids are nicer than the people I tend to meet,

too." Tim was still smiling, the laughter drying up as they looked at each other. "Except for veterinarians, of course. Vets are wonderful."

"You might want to change that statement when you meet my partner." Not that Stacey was mean or nasty, she was just... intense and bossy.

"I don't think I'm going to feel quite the same about her, anyway." Tim lifted his hand to capture Ben's, then kissed the palm. "She's not my type."

It gave him a little shiver, that kiss. And it looked like Tim did intense, too, the look in his eyes making Ben a little harder. He swallowed. "We should pack our stuff up and go walking or something."

"Or something." Tim kissed his palm again and let him go, then rolled smoothly away. "The basket will be lighter now."

"You want me to carry it for a while? You've gotten stuck with packhorse duty this whole evening." He stood and stretched, reaching up for the sky and going briefly on his tiptoes.

"I got it." Tim's hands were suddenly on him, one petting his belly and the other making sure Ben didn't lose his balance. "I think it might be a short walk, though."

"Mmmm... that's nice." He let his arms down slowly, enjoying Tim's touch. "We could just stroll back to the car." He was ready to cut the public part of this date short.

"I think that would be a good idea." Tim brushed against him, his hand petting and the thick length of Tim's cock rubbing a bit against him. "A really good idea. You grab the blanket."

"You just want to see my butt while I'm bent over," Ben teased as he leaned down and grabbed the blanket.

"Uh-huh." Tim pushed against him once more and then moved away, laughing, to gather everything else into the basket. "It's a pretty amazing butt."

Ben shook his head, not because he didn't believe it, but because it was pretty incredible, having someone so into him. He liked it. He liked it a lot. Of course he was pretty into Tim, too, and that made it that much better.

They walked back to the car a lot faster than they'd walked toward the pond, though they were hardly running. Tim took his hand again as they went along the path through the trees, but he made no suggestions about bushes, not even to tease. It felt a bit like Tim was on a mission.

Just as they arrived at the car, his pocket started vibrating and Ben groaned. "No. Not tonight."

Tim looked at him. "I... what?" He blinked a couple of times and tilted his head to the side.

Kind of like a puppy, really.

Ben dug the cell phone out of his pocket. "It's the clinic," he muttered. He flipped the cell open. "It's Ben, what's up?"

"Car versus puppy." Anna's voice lowered. "It's bad, Doc. Like, really."

Well, shit.

"Okay, we're on our way. Ten minutes. If you can find Stacey, get her to give the dog something for the pain." Hanging up, he turned back to Tim. "Emergency call. I have to get back as quickly as possible."

"Hop in." Tim didn't ask any questions, just unlocked the car with his remote access key and put the basket in back. "Let's go."

Ben tossed the blanket in the back, too, and climbed in, buckling up. His mind was already on the pup they were heading toward, hoping things weren't as bad as all that. Sometimes there was more blood than injury, and it could make you think things were worse than they really were.

Either way, it was going to cut their night short.

"Sorry," he muttered as Tim maneuvered them out of the parking lot.

"Not your fault -- and, trust me, hang around long enough and there will be a trail of broken dates with me due to overtime, cases getting hot, or being called away in the middle of the night because some crackhead thinks he can get off a carrying charge in exchange for telling me something." Tim was driving them rapidly toward the clinic, his eyes on the road. "Hang on, I'm going via Sunrise Drive, to avoid the lights on Maple."

"We've had a bad few nights; it's not usually like this." Although, as the practice grew, they were getting more emergency calls. They were starting to think about possibly bringing someone else on so they could spread the load a little. The problem was, they weren't quite there yet.

"Do you know what this one is?" Tim made a fast turn and sped up again, his car's engine revving. "Is it maybe more poison?"

"No, a dog got hit by a car. It's going to be messy and it's going to be long, so I'm afraid I'll have to say goodnight when we get there." There wasn't even time really for a proper goodnight kiss, and his head was already pushing everything else away so he could focus on the animal in need.

"Okay." Tim nodded and took two more corners, then pulled into the parking lot. "Call me when you can."

"Thanks, Tim. I really am sorry about this." Ben undid his seat belt and leaned over to take a quick kiss. Then he was out of the car, hurrying in to try and save a life.

Chapter Six

Tim logged out at lunch and ran. He didn't usually run at lunch -- he found the showers at the station sucked for actually making him feel clean after -- but the relay was creeping up and his endurance could use the boost.

He ran from the station to the park a few blocks away, and then did a circuit around it a couple of times. Given that he couldn't really take his time, he thought he'd better find a hill or two to fight his way up, so he went west a bit and down a tree-lined street, sticking to the shady side.

He was almost at Ben's clinic before he realized he was heading there, then he had to grin at himself. He'd known all along, of course, but he hadn't consciously chosen to go there. But now he was, so he had to decide if he was going to go in or not. It was lunchtime, but he thought that might not make any difference in Ben's schedule.

Amy would love a chance to make him cool his heels, though.

Grinning to himself, he sped up and sprinted into the parking lot, then slowed to an easier pace as he approached the door. He was a mess; breathing hard and sweating wasn't exactly his best look.

"Good afternoon, Amy," Tim said as he went in, making sure to smile broadly.

She looked him up and down, lip curling in obvious disapproval. "He's not here."

"Oh. When do you expect him back?" Tim ignored her look and kept on smiling.

"He won't be back until tomorrow morning."

"And I don't suppose you'll tell me where he is?" Fat chance.

"I can't give out that kind of information." Oh, she did outraged really well. Her voice had risen enough to draw attention to them from everyone in the waiting room. And, it seemed, in the back, too.

A redhead in a lab coat came up behind Amy. "Is there a problem here?" she asked.

"I don't think so, no." Tim smiled at Amy through gritted teeth, and then looked at the redhead. "Amy isn't standing in the way of an active investigation this time, she's merely protecting her boss' privacy. And she doesn't like me." He offered his hand. "You must be Stacey. I'm afraid Ben's never told me your last name, Doctor."

"Oh, you're the cop." Stacey shook his hand, the grip firm and sure. "Ben's barely told me anything about you. Why don't you come around back to my office, and I can give you the third degree?"

He wasn't entirely sure that she was joking.

"Yes, ma'am." He resisted the urge to stick out his tongue at Amy and followed along. "Although, to be completely honest, I'm not here on business this time."

"No, I would have guessed that by your outfit. Unless you're undercover?" She didn't actually go into her office; instead she leaned against the doorway, crossing her arms over her chest and looking him up and down. She wasn't very big, but she had an air of authority and confidence about her that more than made up for the lack of height.

"Nope." He shook his head and grinned. "Just training. I was in the area on my run and thought I'd stop in and see Ben for a moment or two. Amy declined to tell me where he is." Dr. Stacey was far more alpha than Ben, which Tim thought was kind of interesting.

"She doesn't like you, huh?" Stacey grinned and gave him a wink. "You're screwed."

The intercom in her office buzzed. "Lizzie Bellam and her schnauzer Ricky are in waiting room three."

Stacey cackled. "Very screwed." She patted his arm. "Don't let her bother you. And Ben's at his place. I'm guessing you know where that is." Without waiting for the answer to that, she walloped his arm in what he *thought* was meant to be a friendly punch, and headed off down the hall, turning into what had to be exam room three.

He waited until she was gone before he allowed himself to rub his arm. He did not let himself mutter so much as an "ow." "I wonder if I can get her on my relay team?" He shook his head and gave up the thought, then walked back to the desk. "See you, Amy. Have a good day. I'm going upstairs now."

She declined to answer him, picking up the phone, which he hadn't heard ring. "Good afternoon, Terry Road Veterinary Clinic; how may I help you?"

Laughing softly, Tim turned on his heel and went out the front door, and then around to the back. He knew he shouldn't antagonize her, but it was just so damn easy. He'd try to stop before Ben had to tell him to. Maybe.

Around back, he ran up the stairs, his body cooled off enough that his shirt was sticking to him and feeling a bit gross. He hoped Ben didn't mind disgusting cops turning up on his doorstep. When he knocked at the door, he could have sworn he heard Tippy greeting him.

He was about to knock a second time when the door opened, Ben blinking at him. Bed-head was a good look on Ben, and the hole-y sweats and ratty T-shirt were actually kind of sexy. "Tim! Hey." Ben gave him a sleepy half-smile.

"Hey, you. Tough night?"

Ben scraped a hand over his face. "Yeah. Spent four hours trying to save the dog and in the end..." Ben shook his head. "He was hit pretty hard. Hit and run, too. Asshole."

Tim winced. "I'm sorry. People suck."

"Yeah, well. You're not in your uniform."

Tim looked down. "Nope. Lunch hour. I was running and stopped by, but you look like you could use a few more hours sleep."

"Yeah, though I'm awake now if you wanted to come in for a bit."

"I don't have long." But there he was, walking in and taking a nice long sniff of sleepy man. Ben smelled great, fresh out of bed. Better than "jogging cop," anyway.

Ben closed the distance to bring their lips together, the kiss soft and sleepy.

That was nice. Tim approved, and showed it by moving a bit closer, his fingers going to Ben's hair. He didn't want to push too close; he was, after all, sweaty and damp.

Ben's arms went around him and then dropped away. "Ew. Man, you're sticky."

Tim nodded and made a face. "Sorry. I was running, like I said."

"You want a drink or anything?" Ben led him to the kitchen, pulling out one of the chairs at the little table for him to sit on.

"Water would be good." Tim sat and watched Ben move around the room, the sun spilling in the window. "I met Stacey."

"Oh-ho! And how did that go? She grab your balls and ask you to cough?"

"No, that would be Amy." Tim rolled his eyes. "Stacey did tell me I'm screwed, though. And she gave me a friendly punch on the arm. That's good, right? Plus, where Amy had a heart attack when I asked where you were, Stacey told me and even suggested I already knew my way up here." He waggled his eyebrows. "I think I have a chance with her."

Ben gave him a tall glass of water and put on the kettle on, leaning against the counter. "Stacey'll like you well enough as long as you aren't a shrinking violet. What did you think of her?"

"I think she hits hard, that she's strong enough to take care of herself -- physically and mentally -- and I think she's maybe in charge downstairs." Tim wasn't sure if he should have said that last part. "She's no nonsense, but still friendly."

Ben laughed. "She's top dog no matter where she goes, that's for sure." Ben took down a mug out of the cupboard and put a tea bag in it. "She's a really great vet, though. And a loyal friend."

"Good." Tim nodded and tried not to get distracted by the holes in Ben's sweats. "Everyone needs someone like that."

"Yeah. I need a sit down with her this evening. Kind of decompress from last night." The kettle whistled, and Ben poured the hot water into his mug.

Again, Tim nodded. He decompressed with cops. They got it, they knew the job, they just understood the pressures. There didn't seem to be any reason why being a vet would be different. "Do you do that over ice cream?" he asked with a wink. His water glass was getting a film of condensation on it, so he picked it up and drank.

Ben chuckled, but shook his head, bringing his tea

over to the table. "Nah. We stay in with a bottle of wine. Sometimes two."

"So, you're going to be all loose and a bit drunk later? Cool." Tim toasted him with the glass. "I'll be sure to call."

"Horndog."

"I seem to be, don't I?" His grin grew and he shrugged. "I'm sure I can control it if I try harder."

"Oh, don't do that on my account." Ben's eyes twinkled at him.

Tim leered and eyed the rips in Ben's shirt. "All right, I won't."

That had Ben laughing, foot sliding along his leg.

"Hey, last time we played footsie, we were in public. This is nicer." Tim let Ben's foot wander wherever it wanted to go. "Will you be having dinner with Stacey, too?"

"Yeah, I imagine we'll make an evening of it." Unfortunately, Ben's foot didn't wander any higher than his shin.

Oh, well. It wasn't like he had a lot of time to hang out, anyway. "I'll probably eat at my desk." Tim finished his water and set the glass back on the table. "But it's okay if I call you? Or maybe you should call me, when you're done decompressing."

"I don't know, Tim; it could get late. Especially if one bottle becomes two. How about we plan to meet up tomorrow after work?"

Tim did a quick mental review of his calendar. "I think that'll be fine. The afternoon after work, I have a thing with some of the guys -- just more training stuff -- but tomorrow night is clear." He nodded and stood up. "I should go. I have to run back to the station, and I've already eaten my shower time."

Ben got up, too, and came around, tugging Tim close

despite the grossness. "I'll be less out of it tomorrow night, promise."

"You're not out of it." Tim kissed his nose. "You're tired. You worked hard, you need to rest. Like I said last night -- it'll be the other way around, given time."

"Thanks for being so understanding." Ben gave him a proper kiss and then swatted his ass. "You'd better go before you're out of time to have something to eat, too."

"I'll eat at my desk. Again." Tim laughed and headed to the door. "It's the way things go. Call me tomorrow, okay? So we can make plans. All my numbers are on that card I gave you."

"I know." Ben followed him and Tippy looked up from her corner on the couch, giving him a soft woof.

"Later, Tippy." Tim waved to her and then kissed Ben one more time before opening the door. "Get some rest. I'll talk to you soon."

"Yeah. Thanks for dropping by -- it was a nice surprise."

Tim laughed softly and left, going quickly down the stairs. At the bottom, he turned and looked up. "One of these days it'll be nicer."

"I hope so." Ben grinned and waved and closed the door.

Tim smiled to himself and started jogging back to work, pleased with himself. He was halfway there before it occurred to him that he'd forgotten to antagonize Amy one more time. Maybe that was good, though; he probably wasn't amusing anyone but himself with it.

He wanted to amuse Ben. Oh, yes, he really did. With that in mind, he headed to work, hoping the next day would leave him with a lot of energy and a good mood.

Chapter Seven

Ben decided to make supper instead of ordering out.

Of course, by the time Tim was due, he was regretting the choice.

He not only burned supper, but he'd done a bad enough job of it that he set off the fire alarm. Which, to keep the clinic up to code, was actually linked in with the clinic's system. So the sprinklers had gone off, too, and the firemen had been called in.

He was just saying good-bye to them, hunky, studly men down to the last one, when he saw Tim pull up out of the corner of his eye. Oh, man, he had a hunch he wasn't going to live this one down.

Big, tall and buff Steve shook his hand. "Try not to burn any more water."

Ben felt his cheeks heating. "Hey, there were potatoes in there with the water..."

"Maybe you should just give up cooking altogether." Reggie was already up in the driver's seat. Ben would have given the man the finger, except he was Reggie's family vet, and it didn't seem right to give the finger to the man who brought his six-year-old girl in with her various pets.

"I'll take it under consideration." His cheeks were still pretty much the color of the engine as he waved it off down the street, Tim coming up to him. "Hey," Ben managed without sounding too sheepish.

Tim was wearing a huge, shit-eating grin. "Did you know that the police routinely listen in on the radio chatter from the fire department? Part of small town life, really. And did you know how much gets said over those radios?"

"Oh, God." Never, ever living it down.

Tim held out an arm to him. He looked a lot less sticky than he had at lunch the day before. "Aw, poor honey. Still, it was kind of like fair warning that I'll be having take-out. Where should we order from this time?"

Ben went in for the hug and decided on a question of his own before he answered Tim's. "So what exactly got said?" he asked, taking Tim's hand and leading him to the back stairs.

"Well, the initial call got things moving because of the animals. Then it got coded as a kitchen fire. Then there was giggling, talk of a hot date ruined, a list of what you'd tried to cook, and how someone needed to show you how to use a timer." Tim squeezed his hand in what might have been sympathy, except he was still grinning like a fool.

Ben knew his color was at an all-time high. "Giggling? Those big, studly firemen were *giggling*?"

"Well, maybe not giggling. Laughing, yes." Tim looked at him. "Studly? Who's my competition?"

"Did you *see* those guys? Firemen are hot."

Tim rolled his eyes. "Never say that to a cop. Especially one who's gearing up to race them."

"Oh, damn." Ben bit his bottom lip. It was hard to

feel too badly, though, because those firemen *were* hot. But no competition for Tim in the Ben-race department. "Sorry?"

"You can prove you're sorry by kissing me," Tim suggested, sounding hopeful.

"When we get inside." The neighbors were probably still at their windows from the fire truck showing up. God, all he'd wanted to do was make a nice meal, and then he'd gotten distracted.

Tim let go of his hand and bounded up the stairs to wait for him. "It's been a few days," he said with a shrug.

"You were here yesterday at lunch," Ben pointed out. Still, it felt good, knowing how eager Tim was. It made him feel sexy and attractive.

"Ah, but the kissing was minimal and I was disgustingly damp." Tim waited for him to open the door. "This time, there's less sweat -- so far -- and you're awake. Also, revved up by fire fighters."

Ben threw his head back and laughed. "Are you saying I should burn something just before every date?"

"No, because I hear gossip, too, and they'll start trying to figure out who you've got a thing for."

"Oh, the thing I have isn't for a firefighter." He gave Tim a quick kiss and went to open some windows. "Excuse the slightly overdone scent."

"Not a problem." Tim followed right along. "Why don't you tell me about the thing you do have, then?"

"Fishing?" Ben asked, grabbing the take-out menus and handing them over once he'd opened all the windows. "Guest's choice."

Tim didn't even glance at the menus. "Is the host on one of these?"

"You can't have dessert before you have your main meal." If he hadn't skipped lunch, Ben would have been singing a different tune. But then, there was supposed to be a delicious roast with all the fixings for supper.

"Pizza. That's fastest, right?"

"Horndog." He had a feeling that was going to be his private nickname for Tim. "So what do you like on yours? And no, I'm not on the toppings menu. And neither are you."

"Rats." Tim looked over at Tippy. "Pepperoni, brie, and feta okay with you?"

Ben looked at Tim in horror. "Are you serious?"

"God, no. If there's brie on a pizza it better have pear slices with it."

"Oh, thank God. Don't do that to me." He thumped Tim's in the arm.

"Feta needs kalamata olives."

"I'm not putting olives on my pizza. And I'm not letting you do it, either. Not in my sight, anyway." He shook his head. "How about an old fashioned combination -- pepperoni, mushrooms and green peppers. You know, *normal* pizza toppings."

"That'll work. You'll eat fast, right?" Tim crowded into his space, looking that tiny bit up at him. "Please?"

He stroked Tim's cheeks and slid his arms around the man's waist. "Eating fast gives you indigestion," he pointed out, his lips moving against Tim's.

"Eating slow will give me blue balls." Tim kissed him, his tongue darting out to lick and taste.

Ben laughed as he kissed Tim back.

Tim's hands slid down to his ass and squeezed. "Better order soon," Tim said, nuzzling into his neck. "Or I'll start dessert."

"Mmm... we do that and we'll never eat and you'll have to call the EMTs 'cause I'll have fainted. I think one emergency vehicle on the premises in a day is more than enough." He stepped back reluctantly and picked up the phone, ordering them a large combination, with bread sticks and dip.

Tim went over to say hello to Tippy, talking to the dog in conversational tones about her day and what she'd been up to. He didn't seem to mind that she wasn't even bothering to look at him.

Ben hung up and watched. The truth was that Tippy was old and grumpy, and the fact that she didn't growl at Tim meant she approved. He went over and joined them, playing with Tippy's ears. "Should be here in about twenty minutes."

"I'll do my best not to jump you while we wait, then." Tim smiled at him, and sat down on the end of the couch that wasn't taken up by Tippy. "So, how did it go last night? One bottle or two?"

Ben joined Tim, linking their fingers together. "Two. It got pretty maudlin there for a bit, but it was good to get it out of my system."

Tim nodded like he had an idea what Ben meant. "Do you... I mean, you must lose a lot of pets. Do you do this after most of them? Or is it just the really bad ones?"

"We get together once a month or so, usually after a bad one. I mean, lots of animals are put down from old age, and that's not too bad. It's the ones like yesterday, where you spend hours trying to save them and just can't. Those hurt." And when the owners were kids... that just twisted the knife.

"Uh-huh." Tim's thumb rubbed on Ben's hand. "There's bad days, and then there's awful days. I'm glad you didn't have an emergency last night -- either of you."

"Yeah, me, too. No more poisonings, either, so I'm hoping it was just a coincidence. Something accidentally left where the animals could get to it, not something malicious, you know?" He leaned against Tim; it was nice dating someone who understood about the bad days.

"Well, hopefully I'll find that out for sure. It's hard to figure out things when the victims are pets -- people sometimes don't pay as close attention as they would with people. Not the owners, I mean, but the neighbors, potential witnesses, that kind of thing." Tim nuzzled him again, this time just behind his ear. "God, you smell good."

"Yeah? I showered before I tried to cook. Or maybe it's just the contrast with the smoke in the air." He slid his hand to the back of Tim's head, encouraging him to stay where he was.

"I think it's your shampoo. And you." Tim nuzzled again and kissed his neck, then did it again. "Yeah, you."

"Mmm... feels good." It tickled a little, too, but not enough to be annoying.

"Tastes good," Tim murmured, and the kisses became interspersed with delicate little licks.

Ben dropped his head back, giving Tim room. The kisses picked up a little and the licking got a bit rougher; Tim moved, too, and made a low sound. "You're warm," he said indistinctly, and the next kiss included the subtle scrape of teeth.

Ben made a noise, half gasp, half whimper, his cock more than a little happy at the licks and bites. "You're hot," he gasped out.

"Getting that way." Tim kept on kissing and nipping as he made another soft sound. "Oh, man." He moved restlessly and kissed a trail along Ben's jaw. "No marks above the collar. I always have to stop myself."

"Did I say that?" Ben asked. He couldn't remember talking about it.

"No..." Tim looked at him. "But you might want to. About now, maybe."

"Um... I don't think I mind."

Tim grinned. "Fantastic." He nuzzled again and pulled away once more. "I can't have them, though. Uniform and all. Just so you know." Then he dove back in, once more pressing kisses and licks to Ben's throat.

Ben laughed, fingers sliding over Tim's short hair, finding and tracing one ear, then the other. His eyes closed and he concentrating on enjoying it. The drag of teeth with the next kiss became the sharp pull of sucking, Tim's tongue rubbing a bit on the tender skin. It wasn't the only thing rubbing; Tim's hand was kneading Ben's thigh like a cat would. A part of him wanted that hand to move over, but he knew if they started that, they'd be all embarrassingly hot and heavy by the time the pizza turned up.

As it was, when Tim eased off his neck for a moment it was only to kiss him deeply, invading and pushing a groan into Ben's mouth. Maybe a break was needed, for the sake of the delivery guy if nothing else. Ben let his tongue tangle with Tim's for a moment and then pulled away, hands moving to push at Tim's chest. "Enough for now, man."

Tim nodded, his breathing rough. "For now," he said, apparently agreeing. It was just as clear that he had big plans for "later," though.

Ben cleared his throat and moved over a little, putting some space between them. "So, how was your day?"

"Nowhere near as good as the last few minutes." Tim ran his hand through his hair and stretched his legs out, his cock a very impressive lump in his jeans. "Um, it was okay. Court on Monday, so I mostly sat around until the lawyers could go over my testimony. And did a lot of paperwork. You?"

"No dead pets today. Made it a good one." Ben's fingers itched to slide over that bulge and to trace Tim's muscles. Soon, he told himself.

"Sounds like. Was Amy pleasant?" He grinned at the last comment and rolled his eyes. "Man, she does *not* like me."

"Oh, please, the feeling's obviously mutual."

"Maybe." Tim didn't look repentant at all. "I might possibly be used to my uniform being respected, if not me."

"And she's used to ruling the waiting room. I'm not saying it's right, I'm just explaining where it's coming from."

Tim nodded. "Yeah, I hear you. I do. It's thrown me off my stride, really. Not many people get rude to cops unless they're looking for trouble, and she isn't -- I know that. She's just really, really territorial." Tim's grin grew and he poked Ben in the side. "Maybe she spends too much time around animals."

"Yeah, could be." Ben chuckled and shook his head before giving in and leaning forward to press their mouths together.

Tim kissed him back, not as intensely as he had been, but he wasn't being shy, either. Ben could feel Tim smiling, too, which was kind of a funny feeling when kissing, but fun. He focused on the fun instead of the heat, because all the reasons why this should wait until they were done with their pizza still held true. Ben broke away and stroked his thumb along Tim's lower lip. "That pizza needs to get here fast."

"It so does. Are we to the stage of making out for a couple of hours yet? Third date. Fourth? Something." Tim kissed him again and then let him go, though apparently reluctantly.

"Well, we've already had an emergency today, thanks to my attempt at impressing you with my cooking prowess, so I think that bodes well for lack of emergencies later tonight. Of course, now that I've said that..." He reached over and rapped on the coffee table. "Touch wood."

Tim stared at him for a moment. "You know, I'm well aware it's a cheap joke, but I honestly don't care how juvenile it makes me look." He grabbed Ben's wrist and dragged his hand into Tim's lap. "Wood for you to touch."

Ben groaned and turned his hand, sliding it along Tim's erection through the material of his jeans. He squeezed it and petted it and held on for a minute.

Nice.

More than nice.

"Oh, *man*." Tim moaned, and pushed up into his hand. "That pizza better get here *now*." Tim's skin flushed, and his eyes had gone dark and smoky looking.

Ben knew he needed to take his hand off Tim's goods. He really did. Because that pizza was due any minute now. He watched as he squeezed again, the heat of Tim's cock beginning to seep through the heavy denim. He finally yanked his hand away, giving Tim a sheepish smile. "Sorry. But you did start it."

"I know!" Tim was beginning to look a little dazed. "And I'm going to finish it, too."

"Yeah, just not right now." Ben got up and went over to his stereo, looking for a CD to put on. The place still smelled smoky, though it wasn't as bad as it had been. The open windows helped. He could feel Tim watching him, and he was unsurprised when Tim shifted on the couch, then stood up.

But instead of going to the door to see if the pizza guy had arrived, Tim came over to study the CDs. "What kind of music do you listen to most?"

"Rock 'n roll. Chuck Berry, Elvis, the Beatles, Motown. I've got other stuff here, too, but the rock 'n roll is my favorite, what I come back to the most." It was the music he'd grown up on -- his mother's music, and he'd never gotten out of the habit of listening to it.

"Old style." Tim sounded thoughtful as he flipped through a couple of discs. "You know, there's been some neat stuff since. Jazz and blues, and even some fusion with the Motown sound. I don't listen to a lot of stuff that's out, but some of it's good." Tim might have been talking music and trying to maintain a conversation, but Ben couldn't miss the way Tim had to adjust himself, too.

"I know there's been stuff out since the fifties and sixties, Tim. This just happens to be what I like best."

Tim grinned at him. "I wasn't putting it down, man. Really."

"No? That's good. I might have to dump you if you dissed my music." He winked, choosing a compilation CD and sliding it into the player.

"Never happen." Tim's hands lifted, palms out in mock surrender. "Now, I get mouthy about other things, but not a man's music."

"What do you get mouthy about, then?"

Tim laughed. "It depends on my mood, how many hours I've been awake, and if I'm hungry. Mostly I whine about how stupid most TV shows are."

"Oh, I like 'em stupid. The more brainless, the better. Now, ads? Those I talk back to and make fun of."

There was a knock at the door and Ben headed that way, digging into his pocket for cash.

"Oh, thank God," he heard Tim say. "Hey, Tippy. Dinner's here. You know what that means, right? Eating, and then music and kissing."

"Hush, now." Ben shook his head and opened the door, exchanging money for the large pizza box, tipping nicely.

When he turned around, his arms full of pizza box, Tim was right there to take it from him. "I know, I know.

Don't eat too fast. But we don't need to slow down for plates or anything, do we?"

Ben shook his head. He'd laugh at Tim, except he was feeling exactly the same way. "Let me just grab a couple napkins and some water."

Tim nodded and took the pizza to the table. "You know, I'm usually a little smoother than this. But you've got me all turned around and... well, like this."

"Yeah, well, you've got me pretty hot and bothered myself, so I guess we're even." Ben grabbed the bottles of water out of the fridge and some paper towels to use as napkins, and then headed back to the couch. His stomach growled as Tim opened the pizza box and let out the smell.

"Oh, man. Just perfect." Tim lifted out a slice and grabbed a paper towel. "And hot enough that it might slow me down."

"Make sure you take your time. It would suck if stomach cramps from eating too fast ended our evening early." He had plans. The same plans he'd had the night he'd been called into surgery, but that was because they were good plans.

"Hell, I'm only going to eat enough to keep body and soul together." Tim flashed a happy smile at him and made his slice vanish in a few fast bites before reaching for another.

They didn't talk much as they ate, concentrating on filling their bellies. Ben watched Tim as he ate, though, watched the pretty white teeth tear into the pie. He watched Tim swallow and the man's pink tongue come out to drag through the grease left on the side of his mouth.

"I think I'm about done," Tim said, reaching for a water bottle. "I sincerely hope you are, too."

"Nearly." He finished up his last slice and closed the

box as he grabbed it and took it out to the kitchen. He didn't want to tempt Tippy into going for it. Once there, he washed his hands and his face to get the grease off.

He could hear Tim trying to convince Tippy to vacate her end of the couch. "You know, it's not like you *need* to use that space. And I promise you can have it back when we're done."

"I should probably let her out into the yard, anyway. It means we'll have to let her back in again in about fifteen minutes, though." He opened the door and whistled. "Come on, Tippy. Time to take a leak."

She woofed and took her time, stopping for ear scratches from him before she ambled on out, taking the stairs like a pro.

"I can do a lot in fifteen minutes." Tim was right there, reaching for him. "She'll really be okay out there on her own?"

Ben leaned out to make sure she'd gone into the fenced in area through the doggy door, and he nodded. "She'll do her business, play a little, and then come back when she's ready to come back in. She's never tried to run away -- the fence is more to keep people out."

Tim looked through the window at the same time as his hands were sliding around Ben's waist. "Cool. Wanna make out?"

"Yeah, I do. Kind of a lot. A really lot." He closed the door and led Tim back to the couch. "Be a shame not to use it, seeing as we went to the trouble of moving Tippy off it."

"You're brilliant." Tim sat, bringing Ben down with him. "It's a nice couch." Then his mouth was on Ben's again, and Tim pressed a lot closer than he had been before.

Ben opened right up, his hands going to Tim's shoulders, sliding over them and along the well-muscled arms. He had to admit, all that working out paid off. In spades.

"Oh, better." Tim eased them back on the couch, still kissing and touching Ben as they rearranged themselves. "So much better." One of Tim's hands had found Ben's ass.

Groaning, he pressed into Tim, their cocks bumping together, and his only thought was, *Too many clothes*. He couldn't seem to make his fingers do more than feel Tim up, though. And who could blame him? There was lots to feel.

Tim made sounds against Ben's mouth, and his hand was squeezing and guiding. He could feel Tim's cock, just as hard as before, if not harder. They rubbed, and Tim's chest lifted rapidly as he started to breathe faster. "God, yes," Tim whispered between one kiss and the next. "You feel so good."

"So do you." He dove back into another kiss, making out with Tim, just as happy as could be that they were finally doing this.

"Move a little..." Tim gasped as soon as he'd shifted Ben an inch to the right. "God. Yes, right there. Hang on." Tim's hands were everywhere, from Ben's ass to his hair, and Tim was almost writhing against him. "Ben. Yes."

"Yeah. Good. Yes." He wasn't making much sense, but that didn't really matter.

The knock at the door sounded like a shot going off, and Ben gasped and jerked.

"Yoo-hoo! Ben, honey, open up, my hands are full."

Stacey.

Just what he needed.

Groaning, Ben dragged himself off Tim.

Tim scrambled to his feet, his eyes wide. "What? Huh? Oh, crap."

Another knock came, more impatient-sounding this time, as Ben tucked his shirt back in and ran his hands through his hair, aiming at some sort of close relation to normal.

"I mean it, Ben. I can't get the door myself. Don't make a lady wait."

"I'll be.... God!" Tim fled to the bathroom.

Ben sighed, and yelled out "Coming!" as he made his way to the door. He opened it up, Tippy slipping right in and heading for her corner of the couch.

Stacey stood there, bottle of wine in one hand, cake box in the other. "'Bout time, what were you doing, canoodling on the couch?" At his blush, she hooted. "You were!"

He rolled his eyes and stood back to let her in.

"Well, I figured you wouldn't have any dessert. What with the sprinklers going off downstairs and the fire engines and all. Besides, I met your young man, very briefly, and I think it's about time I got to know him a little better, don't you think?"

He just blinked at her. He couldn't believe this.

"Oh, hello, Stacey." Tim rejoined him, looking like he'd splashed water on his face. "Sorry about making you wait at the door."

She gave them both a knowing look. "I'd say sorry for interrupting, but I'm not, really. It's not like this isn't your fifth or sixth date, after all."

"Third, actually. And the last was interrupted by that emergency."

She cackled, her laughter filling the room, and patted his arm before making her way to the couch and sitting in the middle. "Well, I brought cake from the good bakery on Miller's Road. And this is nice wine. So get us some plates and glasses, Ben, and I promise not to grill Tim here too hard."

Ben resigned himself to an evening of blue balls, and went to get the stuff out of the kitchen.

Tim followed right along. "Is she serious?" he whispered, holding onto Ben's elbow. "She's really going to stay?"

"Take a look at her -- she's planted on that sofa harder than Tippy. And she sprang for cake and wine. She's staying." All evening long, too, if he knew her.

"But..." Tim looked baffled. "There was... us. You and me. Couch. Why is she *here*?"

"She's not trying to be a bitch or anything, Tim. She cares about me, and she just wants to get to know you." Ben shrugged. He'd bet that cake of hers that she also assumed they'd already hit a home run or two before now, and that, while she might be interrupting, she wasn't putting them out that much.

He couldn't think of a graceful or polite way to tell her it wasn't so, though. So he figured they were just going to have to live with it. "Grab some forks, will you?" He took three wine glasses out of the cupboard, along with three plates, and headed back in. "Oh, that looks delicious." The cake was covered in white icing and had white chocolate shavings on it, as well as slivered almonds and raspberries.

Tim look a little longer than Ben really thought a simple grabbing of forks needed, but when he came out he was smiling pleasantly. "It really does," he agreed, checking out the cake. "Bit fancy for after pizza, but I think we'll manage."

Ben handed Stacey the bottle opener and started cutting the cake into nice-sized pieces. If Tim was worried about it, he could work out more tomorrow.

Stacey poured their wine, handed Tim his glass, and then hit him with her penetrating stare. "So, Tim. Tell me about yourself."

And thus the grilling began.

It was going to be a long evening, Ben could tell. He had a great view, though, and he smiled at Tim. At least they were both in the same room, instead of one of them haring off to an emergency.

That was good enough for him.

Chapter Eight

Tim checked his time as he ran, and frowned. He wasn't a lot off his personal best, but it was enough to make him worry.

The day was nice and warm but not hot. He'd been sure to hydrate well. The only thing that was really off with him physically was that he'd had a hard time falling asleep. He'd left Ben's place with Stacey, who almost escorted him to his car -- cheerfully, though, so that was okay -- and then had gone home to his empty apartment and emptier bed.

Frustration seemed to be slowing him down.

"You can do better than that!" one of his teammates yelled as he crossed their makeshift finish line. "Even Mandy beat you!"

Tim flipped them all off. Mandy was a regional cross-country champion; she beat *everyone*.

He caught a bottle of water tossed at him and drank most of it. "How slow?" he asked their captain, who was acting as timer for the training session.

"Not that bad, Tim. Less than thirty seconds off your last time. You'll do okay."

Tim rolled his eyes and went to find his bag, hoping he still had a granola bar in there. He'd eat after he did some cool down, maybe, and watch the others.

There was a figure in the distance, heading their way. The guy looked enough like Ben that Tim pretended it was. It would be great to have Ben come watch the rest of his training, maybe go catch some lunch somewhere nice.

Wait a minute, that *was* Ben.

Tim looked down at himself and groaned. One of these days he wouldn't be disgusting *and* they'd be able to hang out. "Hey, you," he said as Ben got near. "What are you doing here? Not that I'm complaining, mind you."

"I have the day off and I was hoping to catch you in action. Looks like I'm too late, though."

"You didn't miss much. I was off my pace." Tim shook his head and reached for his bag. "I think it's Stacey's fault," he said, hoping Ben would know he was teasing.

Ben did laugh, hand brushing over his for a brief moment. "I'd like to see you say that within earshot of her. I bet she could help you run *much* faster."

"Hey, that's a great idea!" Tim beamed at him. "Maybe we should invite her on relay day. So. Do you think I passed, last night?"

"Yeah, I do. She called me this morning to tell me she liked you." Ben looked smug and pleased.

"Thank God. Maybe next time she'll let me actually get to second base."

Ben chuckled, the sound rueful. "I sure as hell hope so. I'm beginning to think I'm never going to get any."

Tim looked around at where his teammates -- his coworkers -- were talking and waiting for the next runner, sitting around and not paying any attention. Then he looked back at Ben. "Want to see my place?"

"Yes. Maybe we won't get interrupted as much there."

Ben's eyes were practically eating him up.

"The chances of Stacey arriving are nil." Tim threw his bag over his shoulder and waved to his team. "See you later," he yelled, heading toward to the parking lot. "Did you drive?"

"I did. You need a lift, or should I follow you?"

"Follow, okay?" Tim pointed to his car and then toward the general area where he lived. "It's not hard to find, and I promise not to lose you."

"You'd better not. I don't think I really want to have to wait another day." Ben's eyes were fixed just south of Tim's belt.

"Not even an hour. Shower with me."

"It seems kind of wrong to jump straight from a few kisses to naked in the shower together."

Tim blinked. "Are you serious?"

Ben blushed and looked away. "I kind of am."

Tim blinked again. "Oh. Okay." He pointed to his car again. "Follow me. But you pretty much have to know I'm totally going to jerk off in there, then. The shower, I mean. Not the car."

"I was hoping you'd just be really quick and then we could get horizontal together..." Ben pulled his keys out of his pocket, moving toward the little red car parked near the path.

"Or that!" Tim almost sprinted to his car, suddenly moving faster than he had all morning. Horizontal was okay, but naked wasn't. Or at least not naked in the shower. Interesting. Slightly odd, and definitely not what Tim was used to, but interesting.

He pulled out of the parking space and made sure Ben was behind him, then made his way home. He was more relaxed following criminals than he was on that drive, obsessively making sure that Ben was still with him after every traffic signal.

At his building, he parked and waited for Ben to join him. "This way. I've got one on the fourth floor. No ground access and no second story jobs."

"Occupational hazard, I guess." Ben chuckled, looking eager.

"Uh-huh." Tim let them into the building and started up the stairs. "It really is. I try not to make it super-obnoxious, but it's stuff I think about when I lease."

"I bet you like the fourth floor for the exercise, too." Ben's hand ghosted over his ass as they climbed.

"It doesn't hurt." He looked back and grinned. "Stairs are good for a nice butt."

"Well, I certainly can't complain about the results." This time the touch was firmer, Ben humming happily.

Tim made himself move faster -- not to get away, but to hurry them both into the apartment. He nearly reached back to pull Ben up the last few stairs and then down the hall. "Home sweet apartment." Unlocking the door and stepping back to let Ben in, he added, "Make yourself at home. I'll be in the shower."

"Wait." Ben grabbed hold of his T-shirt and pulled him in for a kiss, lips opening his, tongue slipping in. Then Ben backed off. "Don't be too long."

"I won't be." Tim had to force himself to back away. "The living room is right ahead, kitchen to the left. There's my bedroom, the spare room that's full of my BowFlex, and that's about it. Be right back." He dropped his bag, went right into the bathroom, and started the water running.

He didn't bother closing the door, either.

When he came out, wearing little more than his towel, Ben was in the living room checking out his DVD collection, bent over to see the titles on the bottom row, ass high.

"I like that you live upstairs, too." Tim brushed his

hand over Ben's ass and leaned over him. The shower had been good for ridding him of sweat, but that was it. He wasn't in the least cooled off.

Ben straightened and Tim let him, especially when Ben leaned back into him. "The clinic has all sorts of security, so by default, I do, too."

"Uh-huh." Tim slipped his arms around Ben and petted his tummy. "I like your place. Plus, it's got Tippy. If you feel like you need added security, though, feel free to call me."

Ben chuckled and turned in his arms. "I'm going to call you, but not for that." Then there wasn't any more talking because Ben's mouth covered his, the kiss going deep fast.

Once more Tim found his hands full of Ben's ass, and he held on happily, backing them toward the couch. He could feel the line of Ben's cock pushing against him, and he shifted one hand around to the front as they stumbled. He wanted to touch.

Groaning, Ben jerked, pushing against his hand. They sat down hard, and Ben sort of pushed against him, sending him down onto his back. The kissing got more intense then.

Tim had every intention of ignoring any interruptions. He got them lined up the way they had been the night before and started moving, rocking up hard and gasping at the way his towel felt against his cock. "Ben. Don't stop. Please."

"No stopping," Ben agreed, rocking against him. The long-fingered hands slid over his chest, stroking across his nipples and feeling up his pecs.

Oh, Tim liked that. He arched his back to give Ben's fingers more room, and hooked one ankle around Ben's leg. They weren't stopping. They were kissing and feeling and panting, and that was good. With a moan, Tim sought

Ben's neck to leave another mark.

His phone started ringing.

Ben kept feeling him up, breath coming short and sharp.

Tim ignored the phone. It was his landline, not his pager or his cell, so it didn't matter. At all. The only thing that mattered was the taste of Ben's skin and the way terry cloth was tugging and rubbing. If he moved his hand three inches, he could feel the ridge of Ben's cock and give him a squeeze.

"You don't have to get that?" Ben asked as the phone kept ringing.

"The machine'll pick up. I don't need to do anything but this." Oh, God, he hoped it wasn't his mother.

"Cool." Ben's mouth latched onto his right nipple just as the machine clicked on.

Tim groaned and arched, the tugging from Ben's mouth going right to his balls.

"Timothy, are you screening your calls again? This is your mother. A mother knows these things. Pick up, I'll wait. And while I wait I'll fill up your machine with the most annoying family news I can think of. You're on your weight machine thing, aren't you, Timmy? Timothy!"

Tim moaned again for completely different reasons and buried his face in Ben's neck.

"Oh, you're kidding me," Ben groaned. As Tim's mother continued, he could feel Ben's prick begin to deflate.

"I hate her." Tim rolled away and stumbled into the kitchen, his mother still talking. "I really, really do." He reached for the phone, fully intending to give her an earful.

"Oh, well. Maybe you're not home after all," she said cheerily. "Call me, honey! Bye!"

Tim stared at the phone. "One of these days... " He

sighed and rewrapped his towel around his hips. "Well." Damn it.

Ben was sitting on his couch, staring at him. "Man. There's nothing like a call from Mom to ruin the mood. Someone out there has decided that we're not allowed to fuck."

"This really, really sucks." Tim pointed down the hall to his room. "I'm fed up, I'm annoyed, and I'm frustrated. I'm going there. Probably to put some clothes on. Possibly to sulk. Want to go out for food?"

"Yeah, we seem to be allowed to eat." Ben winked at him.

"I'm totally going to get fat. And slow. And my hand is going to cramp up." Tim went into his bedroom and opened the closet, wondering what he could wear that might get him laid within ten hours.

"There's that steak place on Main. The one with the amazing onion rings? It's pretty casual, but really good."

"Not casual enough to allow making out, but okay. I can do steak." Might was well get his meat where he could. Jeans and a shirt it was. Shame, really. He'd even made his bed. "Do you need to go and check on Tippy?"

"Nah, she's out the back and Stacey'll look out for her. We should go back to my place after, though. Oh. If you want to, I mean."

"I want to be where you are and where the phones are turned down and where it's unlikely people will walk in on us." Tim pulled his shirt on and shoved the tail into the waistband of his jeans. "I should warn you, though, that all this buildup is either going to make me self-conscious or blow too fast." He only wished he was kidding.

"Hey, I just might cream my jeans the minute we touch, out of self-defense." Ben grinned ruefully at him. "I don't like to fuck on the first date or two, because I don't want it to be all about the sex and nothing else, but we're kind of getting to the point where it's all about the sex, anyway. Kind of ironic, huh?"

Tim nodded. "It is," he agreed. He kissed Ben softly and whispered, "Can't lie. Want you. But, for your sake, I don't want to just do it to get it done, you know?"

"Yeah. At this point, though, I'm more interested in just getting it done than doing the whole hearts and flowers route. We can make it special the second time around." Ben looked him over. "You look nice; let's go eat."

"And then come back here? Or your place. One car makes it less likely we'll get separated by an act of nature." Tim grinned and pointedly put his cell phone on the counter. "I'm off duty."

"Me, too. It's got to be my place though. For Tippy." Ben looped his arm around Tim's waist. "We could just take the one car if you don't mind depending on me."

"I don't mind that at all." He kissed the side of Ben's head and steered them out of the apartment. "Not one bit."

Chapter Nine

B en was beginning to feel a little desperate.

It wasn't like he'd had anything but his hand for ages and he'd been just fine with that. Hell, he'd been the one to back off their first date or two -- he didn't want to just jump into bed. But, really, it was getting to be more than a little ridiculous.

Emergencies, partners, mothers, and the latest fiasco, an accidental power outage that had forced Tim to leave a date within the first few minutes to go back to work. The downtown core might not be huge, but a blackout still meant that there had to be a whole lot of police visible until power was restored. And, of course, their luck being what it was, that wasn't for five hours, after which Tim had gone home and gone to bed so he could get a few hours' sleep before his next shift. When they'd spoke briefly on the phone, Ben had not made plans with the man, being too frustrated.

It was just as well, because work went a little long. Afterward, he ordered from his favorite Chinese place and indulged in some noodles and spicy shrimp. Then he changed into sweats and his raggiest comfy T-shirt.

Settling in on the couch, he picked up his cell and gave Tim a call.

"Geary." Tim's voice didn't sound cold or anything, but he was definitely all business.

"Oh. Hi. It's Ben. Is this a bad time?" It wouldn't surprise him in the least if it was. Fate seemed to be out to get them.

"Ben!" That was better; that sounded like happiness. "Thank God. Hi. I thought you were working. How are you?"

"Tired. It's been a long day, but I'm settled in for the night and thought I'd give you a call. It was that or bad TV."

"Bad TV will rot your brain. I opted for beer and bad movies."

"Well, then, it's a good thing I called you and that you were home." He settled with the phone between his shoulder and his ear, reaching out absently to pat Tippy's head.

"I'm terrified to go anywhere with you on my mind," Tim said with a laugh. "A piano will land on me or something."

"That would be funny if it wasn't so true." He sighed, his cock perky just from the sound of Tim's voice.

"It makes working hard, since I'm always thinking about you. So on top of watching for the usual things, I have to worry about the weird stuff *and* deal with my pretty much constant erection. People are noticing."

"We just need to catch a break. And get a little relief in." He rubbed his cock absently, liking the way it felt. Hell, if he closed his eyes, he bet it would feel like Tim was right there with him.

He could hear Tim's agreement in his voice. "I could really use some relief. I keep putting it off, for some reason. Hoping that the next time it'll work, maybe."

"I know." He pushed his hand into his sweats, touching himself. He could picture Tim as if the man was right there with him, all those hard-won muscles, Tim's mouth, his eyes. "I want you pretty badly right now," he murmured in a low voice.

There was a long pause. "Ben?" Tim sounded like he'd just caught on.

"Yeah?" His own voice was husky, and all he was doing was holding himself. He'd do more, though. With his eyes closed, it didn't feel too weird. As long as Tim didn't make like it was, he thought he could probably do this. Tim's hands were big, and he imagined it was one of them around his dick, hot and sure.

"Oh, man. Wait for me. Hell, yes." The sounds of fabric shifting, or maybe Tim making himself more comfortable, came over the line. "Are you hard?"

He snorted. "As diamonds, man."

Tim made a pleased sound. "That seems to be happening a lot. God, I was so close to coming all over you last time. I want to hear you. I want to know what you sound like when you come."

"Keep talking like that and you will." The things Tim said made him groan, and he started moving his hand, sliding it up and down along the heat of his cock. Tim would hold him like this, would thrust along his cock and make him feel so good.

"I'm not very good at talking," Tim told him, his breath catching. "I just know what I want. I'm kind of selfish. I want your hand on me. I want to taste you, all of you. And I want to make you yell my name sometime. Mostly I want... oh, man. I want to make it good." There was a definite rhythmic squeak happening somewhere.

"Just getting to come with you would be good." It would be awesome. Hell, this was closer than they'd gotten yet, and he half expected a meteor to land on the house or something.

"Uh-huh. Where are you? I want to picture it."

"Couch. Sitting slumped. Hand down my sweats. I'm pretending it's your hand, though."

"*Fuck*." Tim gasped so loudly Ben could almost feel it. "I've got both hands on me. One on the head and the other on my balls. How do you like it, Ben? Fast and tight? Or slow and steady?"

"Uh-huh, yes." He nodded. He just wanted it, any way he could get it. He'd started out slow on himself, but now his hand was moving faster, Tim's eagerness getting him going. He could hear Tim's breath, and imagined he could feel it against his neck.

"Yes," Tim echoed. "Yes, like that. Oh, man." The squeaking was faster and Tim was breathing hard.

"You in bed?" Ben spread his legs, the phone still wedged between his shoulder and chin, and reached down with his other hand to cup his balls and push them up against his body.

"Chair in the living room. Bed's quieter. *God.* I need lube. Next time, I'm using lube."

Ben only grunted his reply, getting close. He bit his bottom lip, groaning. Tippy suddenly woofed and walked over to his side of the couch, licking his arm and woofing again. "Go away," he growled.

"What?" Tim made a rough sound that was a like a growl. "No one. *No one* is getting in the way of this."

"The dog," he muttered, opening his eyes and growling at Tippy. "Go on, back to your corner. Or food. Kitchen. Come on, Tippy. I just need two minutes."

Tim growled again. "Ben. Ben, I'm close. God, stick with me. Jesus, I wish you were here. I want you here, where I can see you, feel you. I want to suck your cock, Ben. Hear me?"

"Oh, God." He shoved with his arm, getting Tippy to

back off, and then turned so he didn't have to watch those big eyes looking at him. "Just a bit more, Tim. Please, I gotta."

He could hear Tim panting and then a long, low groan. "Ben. Come on, honey. With me. My mouth on you, your cock on me, rubbing, thrusting, your hand on my balls, in my ass -- oh, *fuck*, yes!"

"Oh, God!" He jerked, pushing his cock though his hand and coming hard, heat spraying up over his skin. He pictured it splashing on Tim's ridged abdomen, the lovely muscles covered in his come.

From the other end of the line came more panted breaths, and something close to a whimper. "Oh, man. Yeah."

Ben chuckled, stretching and looking idly for a tissue to clean up with. "We did it!" Not together together, but right now it felt like a triumph.

"Totally. God, there's juice all over the place." Tim sounded pleased with the mess. "I don't think I can stand up."

Ben chuckled. "One reason why I started on the couch instead of a chair. More comfortable."

"Ah, but I thought I was going to watch a movie. I didn't know I was going to get lucky." Tim laughed, too, the sound warm and happy.

Ben finally found the tissues and wiped himself up before sprawling lazily, right where he was. Tippy was back in her corner, eyes closed, looking for all the world like she was already asleep again. "Now we just have to figure out how to do it in person."

"Maybe we broke the spell." Tim sounded vaguely hopeful. "Tomorrow, I've got a double shift. Unless I come by the clinic with new information or to ask more questions, I don't think I'll even see you until.... what? Tuesday?"

"I can do Tuesday. I'm on call, but honestly, while we've had a run of calls the last few weeks, it's usually much quieter." He'd like to think they could actually get together like normal people and not get interrupted. Hopefully, Tim was right; maybe this had broken the spell and they could just move forward naturally.

"So," Tim said slowly. "I guess we should pick a spot. Why don't you come over here? We can try my local pizza place for a change, and maybe put a movie in. If nothing blows up, we can move on from there."

"It's a date. Or... a plan. You think a plan will be less likely to get shot to hell than a date?" He chuckled, feeling nice and sated.

"Oh, I bet it will. You really are very smart. And hot. But I should really go and shower before I get stuck like this."

"Yeah, okay. And I've got some bad TV to watch."

"Stuff will rot your brain. Good night, Ben."

"I'll take my chances. 'Night, Tim."

He hung up and tossed the phone on the coffee table.

Okay.

That was more like it.

Chapter Ten

Tuesday came and went, and Tim was up to his ears in cases and training. He was very pleased that no more pets seemed to have been poisoned, as that indicated there wasn't actually anything malicious going on. There may just have been some tragic neglect somewhere. But it also meant he couldn't even drop by Ben's clinic with an update. They kept in touch by phone as best they could, but face-time was proving elusive.

On Wednesday, Tim worked a split shift, grabbing some overtime when he knew Ben was on call, but by Thursday, he'd had enough. After his day shift ended, he went back to his apartment, did a fast workout, and called the clinic, fairly sure Ben would be just finishing up for the day.

"Terry Road Veterinary Clinic, how may I help you?"

"Hey, hi. I was wondering if I could have a word with Dr. Sauvigon , please."

"He's not available right now; can I take a message for him?"

"Is he in surgery or something?" That would just be

about right. A night off, a sense of determination, and no Ben. "It's Constable Geary calling. He has my numbers, if he's not going to be tied up for hours. Well, tell him to call me anyway, please. I don't care what time it is." Wow, that was pathetic. True, though.

"Yes, Constable, he is in surgery. I'll make sure he gets your message. It might be a while, though, it's a bad one."

Well, the night clerk was certainly friendlier than Amy.

"Okay, thanks. And tell him I said I hoped it went well." Tim sighed and hung up. Then he looked down at his sweat pants and decided that a shower and his hand were going to have to do. Again. "God, this sucks. Or not."

It seemed they were doomed. If he didn't like Ben so much, he'd have given up the relationship as not happening ages ago.

As it was, he was beginning to think they were never going to get past second base while in the same room.

Thursday found Ben exhausted, almost sleepwalking his way through the day after being up most of the night in surgery.

The only saving grace was that the dog had survived; Maggie was recovering in the clinic and, unless there were complications, would be able to go home tomorrow.

He went home at six, set his alarm for nine, and promptly fell asleep.

He slept through the alarm.

He was run off his feet on Friday, and by the time he was able to sit and give Tim a call, it was after six.

There was no answer at Tim's place, or on his cell,

so Ben left a message. He didn't want to call too early Saturday morning, so he waited until it was after ten before trying Tim at home.

"'Lo?" That was the sound of one groggy cop.

"Oh, man, I'm sorry. I thought I'd be safe from waking you up if I waited until now." Shit. Now he felt bad.

"Ben? Hey, you." He could hear Tim yawn hugely. "I worked all night, things were busy downtown. How are you? I was starting to think you'd given up, man."

"No, I've just been busy. Look, I'll let you get back to sleep. What are you doing tomorrow?"

"Working." Tim sighed and made a frustrated sound. "I actually need to train with the team this afternoon, get more sleep, and clock in tomorrow morning at six. Can I call you tomorrow night?"

"Sure, no problem. Sleep well."

There was a pause, and then Tim said, "I miss you."

"Yeah, tell me about it." Ben laughed, but he didn't feel very jolly. They'd joked that they were cursed. It wasn't feeling very funny right now. Before he could get too maudlin, he offered a cheery, "I'll talk to you tomorrow night, 'kay?"

"You got it. Bye, Ben." Tim yawned the last two words and hung up, presumably to go right back to sleep.

Ben stared at the phone for a while and then grabbed Tippy's lead. "Come on, girl. This calls for ice cream."

Tim knew in his heart that the time was finally right. It had to be. After all, it had been more than a week since they'd last actually seen each other, and any longer than that was unthinkable. So he showered before he called, and made sure he had a decent shirt ready for when Ben accepted his invitation to dinner.

Then he picked up the phone and called, sure that it would all work out.

"Hello!" Okay, that wasn't Ben, not unless he'd suddenly turned into a girl.

"Uh." Oh, that was smooth. "I'm sorry, I must have the wrong number. I was calling Ben."

"This is Ben's place. What's your name, honey?"

Tim blinked. "Stacey?" God, it had to be Stacey. Damn it all. "It's Tim. Is Ben around?"

"Tim! You *are* still around! That sly devil -- he hasn't said anything. Ben! Ben, it's your boyfriend."

"Hardly that," Tim muttered. "We'd have to see each other." And, oh, ow. It wasn't a good thing if Ben wasn't even talking about him. Crap.

"Tim? Hey. Just a second." A moment later Ben came on, and there was less noise in the background. "Sorry, had to come out onto the porch. There's a bit of an impromptu party going on. How are you?"

"I'm... You're having a party?" Again, ow.

"No, not really. Well, I guess so. Stacey just picked up the big Watson farm as a client and she wanted to celebrate, so the employees are all here. Good for morale and stuff. I'm sorry, it just sort of happened."

He heard something in the background, and Ben saying, "Yeah, yeah, I'm coming." And then Ben was talking to him again. "Look, I really am sorry, but I've got to go before they shave Tippy or put her in a tutu or something. I'll call you tomorrow."

"Yeah, fine." Tim rubbed his eyes and pinched the bridge of his nose. "You do that. I'll be around." Not like he had anywhere else to be.

""Kay, bye." Ben sounded distracted, and the phone clicked off without anything further.

Great. Just great.

Maybe he wouldn't be around after all. Tim hung up

and went to put on his shirt. He wasn't going to wind up sitting at home alone when he didn't want to.

It was Tuesday night before Ben had a chance to sit down and give Tim a call. He had the whole evening in front of him, though, and he was hoping against hope that he could spend it with Tim.

The phone rang through to Tim's answering machine, and Ben sighed. No, he did not want to leave a message, he wanted to see Tim, damn it.

Wednesday evening found him once again calling Tim, and once again getting the answering machine. This time, he didn't bother leaving a message.

Tim pulled up to the clinic in his patrol car and glared at the doors. He didn't want to be there. He didn't want a dead pet, and he didn't want to see Ben like this. He was tired of telephone tag and he was tired of being put off for co-workers. Emergencies he could deal with -- that was his life, too, after all -- but impromptu parties and friends who wouldn't leave when they were clearly interrupting a date? Screw that.

Plus, it was daytime, and that meant little Miss Bitchy at the desk.

He got out of the car and slammed the door, then headed in, his notebook already in hand. No bullshit this time. This was work.

Amy looked up as he came in and, while she didn't look particularly friendly, she did point to the door to go into the back as soon as she saw him, not even waiting for him to tell her why he was there. "They're in Ben's office."

He nodded his thanks instead of saying it, and went through the door and on down the hallway. Maybe he could just get the information he needed and get out of there quickly. He hoped to hell that they had blood samples he could take with him, too.

At Ben's door, he rapped on the frame and waited for them to look up.

Ben and Stacey looked up at his knock and Ben stood, coming to usher him in and close the door. Ben was pale, Stacey looked furious.

"Three," she said as soon as the door was closed. "Three more poisonings, all from the same area. One came in last night, and we've already had two today. What are you going to do about it?"

Ben sighed and rubbed his eyes. "Stacey..."

"What? What? Aren't you pissed off, Ben? Because I am fucking livid, and what are the cops going to do -- the same nothing much they've already done?"

"Stop it, Stacey. Tim is here to help."

Tim's back went stiff as soon as Stacey opened her mouth. "Do you have blood samples for me, ma'am? And when you're calm, you may tell me what you know."

Her eyes went wide. She opened her mouth, and Ben stepped between them. "I can do you one better than blood samples -- we still have the animals. I told their families we needed them for the police. Come on, I'll show you."

Oh, great. Dead animals. Tim hoped to hell that Ben had some nice boxes he could take them in. He turned on his heel and opened the door, waiting to be led to where the bodies were, and said nothing.

Ben gave Stacey's shoulder a squeeze. "I know you're upset, Stacey, we all are. The yelling thing doesn't help, though. There's a bottle of brandy in my bottom right drawer. I bet that'll work way better than yelling."

Stacey patted his hand and then Ben joined him, leading him across the hall to a storage room. "They're wrapped in plastic and in a box. It was a cat and two dogs this time. All different owners, all within the same general area, but they don't know each other. The closest two live six blocks away from each other. There's no way this was something being accidentally left out." Ben looked haggard, with huge bags under his sad eyes.

Tim nodded and looked at the box. "I'm going to need addresses again, Ben," he said softly. "And I need to know everything the owners told you. Every word. I've got nothing, really, so any rumor, any anger they expressed against a particular person... I need it all so I can make this stop."

Ben nodded. "Yeah. Yeah, I know. I told them that the police would need to come talk to them. The files are back in my office. I put all that information down while it was fresh in my mind. This is..." Ben shook his head and ran his hands through his hair. "Someone is deliberately doing this to pets -- what happens when killing dogs and cats doesn't get them their jollies anymore?"

"Then there's going to be bigger problems." Tim couldn't tell him any differently. "I'm sorry you're facing this. I'm going to have to go to all the other clinics, too, and find out about anything I'm missing. Have you spoken with other vets, given them the heads up?"

"Yeah, I did that after you came in the first time. But I'll call them back and let them know it's gone from a possible rash of poisonings to a definite." Sighing Ben covered the box up, and then leaned against a shelf full of supplies. "You look good." There was a wistful tone to Ben's voice.

Tim gave Ben a long look and closed the door. "You look like crap. Are you sleeping at all?"

"The first poisoning came in last night around ten. I didn't get any sleep last night at all." Ben gave him a sad smile. "And I... well." Ben shrugged. "I know we've only been on a handful of ill-fated dates, but I still miss you."

He couldn't quite not sigh. "Yeah, well. Things aren't exactly going in our favor. And now it looks like I have a hard couple of days ahead of me." But Ben was right there. In front of him. Too bad they were in a storage room.

Ben reached out and touched his belly, just above his utility belt. "You have that charity race against the firefighters this weekend, right?"

"Uh-huh." Unless he got called in. He didn't really think about that, though, not with Ben touching him. So, so close. He was getting hard. "Are you going to come watch?"

"I was hoping I could. Hope Park at noon, right?"

Tim was pretty sure he hadn't told Ben that; he'd obviously gone to the effort of finding out when it was. He nodded, not looking away. "Yeah. That's the start for my leg -- I'm on day two. I'll be there early." He licked his lips, his mouth suddenly bone dry. "I really should go. Um. We should. There's information I need." *Or,* he added mentally, *I'll wind up throwing you against the door right now. That'll really piss Stacey off.*

Ben nodded, fingers curling and then dropping away. "I'll carry the box out to your car."

"Thanks." Tim made himself breathe and hoped to God that his trousers were hiding what he was packing. "The addresses and stuff are on your desk?"

"Yeah. The files are all together." Ben bent to grab the box, and Tim had to remind himself what was in it to keep from rubbing up against Ben's ass.

"Are you -- never mind." He knew exactly what Ben was doing that night, and logically he himself would be working pretty intensely until at least nine or ten. "I miss you."

"Good. I mean, I'm glad I'm not the only one feeling that way." Ben rolled his eyes. "That didn't come out right. Come on, this is surprisingly heavy."

"Next time we try to block out time, tell Stacey to piss off, okay?" There, he'd said it. He'd probably just lost his one remaining chance, probably just ruined everything, but he'd said it.

"Huh? She's not coming to the race with me." Ben looked honestly confused and utterly worn out.

"Good." Tim sighed and let it go. He'd try again later. "I'll grab the files off your desk." He opened the door and hoped to hell that he wasn't about to bang into anyone with it as he moved to let Ben out with the box.

Stacey was coming out of Ben's office, the files in her hand. She offered them over with a tight smile. "I'm sorry, Tim. I know you're here to help, and you didn't deserve the crap I gave you. I'm just so damn angry."

Tim took the files and blinked at her. "I understand," he said, because he did. "It's not easy, and I don't expect you take this stuff well. I'm doing everything I can, I promise."

"You catch him and bring him by here." Man, he did not want to be on the receiving end of the look in her eyes.

"Uh, no." Not that he didn't appreciate the sentiment. "I'll catch him and toss his ass in jail, though."

"Damn it." He was pretty sure she meant it, too. With that, she patted his arm, gave Ben's arm a squeeze, and headed down the hall.

"You want to get the door for me?" Ben asked, nodding to the door that would bring them back to the reception area.

"Uh, sure. She's confusing." He opened the door and

held it for Ben, then went to open the exterior one as well.

"She is?"

"Yes." Tim left it at that, not wanting to get into a debate about Stacey when Ben was running on empty. "How late do you need to work?" he asked as he walked to his patrol car.

"We're booked solid and already behind." Ben shook his head. "It's the longest day in the history of days."

"God." He unlocked the trunk and moved to take the box. "Try to get some sleep, okay? I'll call tomorrow if I have anything to update. Hopefully, a few hours plotting everything on a map and talking to all the pet owners again will get me somewhere. The lab might take longer, but I'll see if they'll rush for me."

"Okay, thanks." Ben passed over the box, hands lingering a moment. Then he stepped back and waved. "I'll see you Saturday. Rain or shine, right?"

"Rain or shine." Too bad the last couple of weeks had pretty much convinced Tim that he'd believe it when he saw it.

He watched Ben head back inside and shook his head. He had a lot of work to do; maybe that would help him with the 'not thinking about stuff he didn't seem able to change' thing he had going on.

With another sigh, one that made him feel like he was a broken record, he got in his car and headed to the lab with the bodies. It was going to be a long day.

Chapter Eleven

B en wasn't sure how you dressed up for a charity run between cops and firemen. It was a run, so he had to figure that casual clothes would work.

But then, it was between very fit *cops and firemen.*

He didn't want to look like a schlub. In the end, he figured Tim wouldn't expect him to be all dressed up, so he found his best pair of shorts and a newish blue T-shirt, sandals, his Iams ball cap, and a smile.

The forecast wasn't the nicest, but it had been sunny so far, and when Ben got to the park, there were already loads of people there. The firemen and cops were out in force to support their teams, wearing their uniforms, carrying signs to slag each other off and going over the results of the first day's race.

In fact, most of the supporters seemed to be firmly in one camp or the other. Ben wandered into "cop" territory and kept an eye out for Tim.

There was a roped-off section with a tent, tables under the awning full of water bottles and boxes of power bars, and two guys pinning numbers onto runners. It looked vaguely like registration and whole lot like where Tim should be. There were a lot of people, though, and it wasn't until a group of chatting supporters moved to the side that Ben saw him, standing by the rope and talking to a man who was clearly going to run, too.

Man, Tim looked good -- he looked fit and muscled and sexy, and Ben grinned and shook his head as his prick made a concerted effort to get involved in the looking. This enforced-celibacy thing was sucking hard.

Hell, he wasn't even a hundred percent sure they were still dating. They'd only had a stolen moment when Tim had come in to the clinic, and he'd only been there for work. He hadn't called since.

Ben sighed and tried to talk himself out of being depressed about things. Hey, at least his prick had gone down at his thoughts.

Tim laughed at something his companion said, and turned his head to look around. Ben wasn't sure what he was looking for, but as soon as Tim saw him his smile grew even wider. "Hey!" Tim waved him over, his hand out. "You came! Ben, this is Keith, he's on my team. Right after me, actually."

Ben went over to them and held out his hand. "Hi, there. Nice to meet you."

Keith shook his hand and smiled at him. "Thanks for coming out." Then he grinned. "Don't forget to make a donation."

Tim rolled his eyes. "Turn it off, man. Go and see if Mandy's around the bend, yet."

Ben chuckled and reached back for his wallet. "You never did hit me up for a donation, man. I assume there's also a rivalry to see which team can bring in more money?" He opened his wallet, wondering what an appropriate donation would be. There had to be a range for... well, boyfriend with hopefully more.

"Man, if we beat them in fundraising it'll be almost

better than winning the race." Tim looked positively gleeful over the prospect. "The race is all about bragging rights and strutting. The money is about not having to organize next year's event *and* bragging and strutting." He grinned at Ben as Keith drifted away. "I'm glad you came. I wasn't sure you would."

Tim's hand reached out and brushed lightly over Ben's wrist.

"Hey, I said I would. I'm not even on call this weekend." He'd had to promise Stacey a huge favor at a date to be named later, which was a little scary, but she'd agreed to be on call, on her own, from Friday night through Monday morning. Ben wasn't sure anything was going to happen, things still felt kind of weird, a little bit awkward between him and Tim, but it was nice to know that if it did, he wasn't going to wind up with blue balls again.

Tim raised an eyebrow. "Not on call. Like, at all? And Stacey isn't camped out on your steps? There's no scheduled clients? No known reason that'll have you running off as soon as I finish the race, even before my heart rate slows to normal?"

"I think answering that question with a yes might jinx it."

"Good point." Tim looked around and nodded. "I have three legs to run. In the first, I'm running third man. In the second, I'm second. The last leg I'm the second to last runner, so I should finish up about three-thirty, if all goes well. Are you going to stick around for it all?"

"Yeah. They're selling hamburgers and stuff, so I won't starve or anything. It should be fun." He looked down at his wallet, which he'd forgotten he'd dug out. "Hey, how much should I donate?"

Tim smiled. "However much you want. It's all good. I'm a bit more interested in what I can get out of you later. Do I get more if we win?"

Ben blinked and then grinned. "I won't be holding back. Period."

Tim's pupils dilated. "I'll hold you to that." He took a small step back and shook his head. "Now I really need to be somewhere where you aren't, so I can stretch and warm up. Hard to run when your blood flow is all messed up."

Heat bloomed in Ben's belly. "I'm going to go find someone to give some money to and see if anyone can tell me a good spot to set up and watch. Good luck!"

"Thanks." Tim was still looking at him intensely. "Cheer loud. I'll hear you." Then he turned and loped off, and Ben could see the black "119" on his back.

Ben watched until Tim was out of sight. Then he turned and started looking for a donation center.

The sky might have started to get cloudy, but the day was definitely looking up.

Tim managed to get himself focused, though it took a bit of work. He really, really shouldn't have convinced himself that there was no way Ben would show up. Seeing him, flirting with him, had thrown him for a loop. But he got it together and ran hard. At the end of the first leg, the police department had a forty second lead, total.

Not nearly enough.

Tim sat with his team and yelled and cheered and drank water and sports drinks. He ate what he was given and he yelled polite abuse at the firefighters. It was a family event, after all. Everyone kept the teasing mostly clean.

He also spent more than a few spare moments looking around to see if he could spot Ben. He saw him a few times, mostly hanging out near the finish line, but he did catch him at a mid-point, cheering madly, during the second leg.

Running so close to the end of the race, Tim had to put everything he had into each step, into every breath. He knew he was running in a pack, but nothing mattered other than going as fast as he could, especially when he came around the final bend and had the straightaway in front of him, the runners for the last leg already lined up.

The crowd was deafening. He ran as hard and as fast as he could, his lungs burning and his legs screaming at him. He felt amazing, endorphins pushing him hard, every step flowing through him as he sprinted toward Keith, the baton a heavy weight. He sensed fewer people around him, but didn't check to see how many he'd lost.

When Tim slapped the baton into Keith's hand and Keith shot away, Tim had to keep running, just a few meters. If he stopped, he'd trip. Gasping for air, pacing to get his heart rate down and knowing he really should do a proper cool down, Tim looked around to see how they were doing.

The first thing he saw was Ben, looking down the raceway after Keith, clapping and bouncing and cheering.

Tim accepted a bottle of something and a lot of back-slapping as he made his way to Ben. He thought maybe they might be doing okay, given the way everyone was jumping around, but then, they'd be jumping anyway. He mopped his face and drank blue stuff, then finally reached Ben. "How was my time?" he asked, grinning at the way Ben looked so excited.

"Hey!" Ben gave him a hug, bouncing with him. "You guys have a huge lead. If Keith can hold onto it, you've won!"

"For real?" Wow. That was pretty awesome. So was Ben, right there and bouncy. "Careful, I'm gross," Tim said with a laugh.

"You are. You need a shower." Ben's eyes were admiring, though, happy and excited.

Tim nodded, already watching the race. He could feel sweat trickling down his back. "Last time I invited you to join me, you said no."

Ben replied in a low voice, quiet enough he almost didn't catch it. "I kind of wanted the first time to be special. Or at least horizontal, you know?"

"I know. But at this point, I'll take anything." Tim rolled his eyes. "Still. Your call, man. All I know is that I need a shower."

"I think turning anything down at this point would be foolish." Ben leaned in. "I'd even take a quick hand job in your car, man, sweat and all."

Tim's ears rang and his blood rushed south. "Ben." He almost didn't recognize his voice, and he sure as hell didn't care about the damn race anymore. "In fifteen minutes there's going to be hundreds of people in the parking lot."

"Yeah, well, we can drive back to mine. Or yours. I'm just saying, I won't be saying no."

"Yours." Tim said it reflexively. "Tippy's been alone a while now."

Ben beamed at him. "I'll meet you there once the race is over."

Oh, right. The race. Tim grinned back and wondered if he could hold his drink bottle just right enough to hide his boner from the world. At least almost everyone seemed focused on the race.

The crowd got louder as the minutes went by, uniformed cops and firefighters crossing into their team areas to help cheer things on. Tim knew about a lot of side bets, and he was pretty sure, seeing the desperation on the FD's faces, that there was going to be a fair number of cars being washed at the station house.

The runners rounded the bend, Keith at the front of the pack, and Ben punched him in the arm. "Look! Look!"

"Well, holy crap." Tim started yelling with the rest, and jumping. When Keith actually sped up, Tim turned to Ben. "I'll get lost in there, but I swear I'll meet you at your place. Then, you're coming with me to the team barbecue. Say yes."

"Yes." Ben looked like he was going to say more, but the group around them surged and they got separated as Keith crossed the finish line ahead of his nearest FD competitor.

Tim joined the crowd, going nuts as they all piled, first onto Keith, and then onto each other. It took a couple of minutes for things to settle down, for them to finish patting each other on the back and spraying each other with water and God only knew what else. That shower was going to be absolute heaven.

Ben. Oh, yes. Tim stuck around for the official word that they'd won, and the announcement of the total amount raised for charity -- the fire department, damn them, had raised more by several hundred dollars -- and then he begged off.

"I swear I'll be at the barbecue," he told Keith. "Save me a beer. I just need to shower first and stuff. I'll be there!"

Keith nodded and waved him off. "You better be."

And with that, Tim was free. He grabbed his gym bag and almost ran back to his car. About three strides into it, he thought better of wasting any more energy, and merely walked.

Quickly.

Chapter Twelve

Ben slipped away soon after Keith crossed the finish line. He figured he'd have less of a traffic jam to sit in, if he left before the bulk of the participants and their supporters. Besides, he wanted to make sure he got there before Tim.

If he could let Tippy out, and find something for them to munch on, and dig out a clean towel before Tim showed up, well, then, if he jumped the man's bones the moment he walked in the door, that would be okay. "It's not a sure thing," he informed his cock. He was still worried about jinxing it.

There were no messages on his machine when he got in, and Tippy waddled happily outside. Ben found a towel and added it to the rack in the bathroom, and he found crackers and cheese and a bunch of grapes that only had a few bad ones on it. Then he went out and tossed the ball a few times for Tippy, full of nervous energy.

When half an hour had passed, he brought Tippy back inside and tried not to fret. He *knew* there was going to be a lot of traffic trying to get out of the place. And Tim had been on the team that won, for Pete's sake. He was probably just being congratulated and stuff.

Ben turned on the TV and flipped through the channels. Then he turned it off and started wandering around the place, going to the window every time he thought he heard a car.

He heard someone dashing up his stairs and then a sharp knock at the door; Tim didn't even wait for him to get there before he opened the door. "Hey," he said as he walked right in. "We won. I'm disgusting. You're hot. Come here."

Ben laughed and deliberately did not run. He wasn't going to attack Tim the moment he walked in -- the man wanted a shower, right? He pushed Tim back against the door, their teeth clacking together as he dove in for a kiss. Okay, he was going to attack Tim the moment he walked in.

Hands landed tight on his ass and Tim yanked him close. God, Tim was hard, even through their clothes. His mouth tasted of something sugary and Tim was kissing him back, hard enough to bruise.

Oh, God, they were kissing and touching and rubbing and he couldn't believe they were actually doing it. He tugged Tim's T-shirt out of his shorts and started to push it up. Then he changed his mind. Fuck it, he wanted the man's cock.

He shoved his hand into Tim's shorts.

Tim gasped into his mouth and broke the kiss as he head fell back. "Ben. Yeah." His hips were thrust out, already twitching when Ben got a hold of Tim's cock. "Please."

It was damp with sweat and so damn hot, skin silky over the hard core. Ben began to jerk it, rubbing himself frantically against Tim's hip.

Tim moaned and panted, one of his hands ineffectually tugging at the button of Ben's shorts. "Let me. You, too.

Oh *God*." His hands stilled and he thrust hard into Ben's hand. "Tighter." The hand still on Ben's ass squeezed, and fingers pressed deep.

Ben wasn't sure if he got his hand any tighter around Tim's cock, but he did jack him faster. He moved his hips faster, too, humping against Tim's leg like a dog in heat.

Tim's eyes squeezed shut and his cock throbbed in Ben's hand. He made a rough sound, just one, and opened his eyes wide. "Ben," he whispered. He'd given up on getting Ben's shorts open, but he had his hand over Ben's cock, and when Tim started to come, he massaged Ben with every pulse that spilled.

Ben moaned, wanting to come so badly. He could feel it gathering in his balls, in his spine. He whimpered when the scent of Tim's come hit him, but his own orgasm didn't happen.

"Fuck," Tim said, making the vowel long and slow. "God." He shook a bit, and then started to slide down the wall. "No, no, let me," he said when Ben tried to keep him up. "Let me take care of you."

"Please, God. I can't..." He gasped. His cock was so hard he hurt; he just couldn't. Fuck.

"Shh." Tim slid to the floor, his hands on Ben's hips, his ass, his cock, all over the place. His hands were working, too, and even though he was still panting, still flushed, Tim got Ben's shorts undone and down, freeing his aching erection. "I'll take care of you," he said softly, just before he started licking.

Ben made an inarticulate noise and reached for the door, hands flat against it. "Please. *Please*." His hips pushed, trying to get friction, heat, something. Tim didn't say anything more, just opened up and took him in, not teasing. He didn't even wait until he'd gotten Ben's cock all wet, just... took him in and started sucking and licking and bobbing his head. Tim's hands roamed, like he couldn't be still even if he had come, touching everywhere.

"Oh, fuck!" Ben's hands landed on Tim's head, holding him in place as he started thrusting, fucking Tim's mouth. He shouted as his balls finally let go, shooting deep into Tim's throat.

Around him, around his prick, Ben could feel Tim swallowing. He took it all, and then he licked and suckled until Ben thought he might fly apart. The hands on his thighs and ass kept on petting, even when Tim finally let him go.

"Jesus," Tim said in a rough whisper. "Tell me you let go like that a lot. Please."

Ben had come so hard he was shaking, not even sure what was keeping him upright. "Um..." He panted, not really able to form words yet.

Tim kissed him. Tim kissed the top of one thigh, then his belly, and then he was struggling to his feet and kissing Ben's mouth, still holding onto him. "I need to shower. And I need you. We're a long way from done, Doc."

He nodded and managed to wave in the general direction of the bathroom. "Can't believe we weren't interrupted."

"Shhhh." Tim kissed him again, smiling. "We're going to get clean and sneak off to a barbecue before that can happen, okay?"

"Not sure I can walk, but sure." He gave Tim a lazy grin and risked standing on his own feet without the door's support. Oh, staying upright. Cool.

"You going to wash my back?" Tim asked with a wink. "You don't need to. But water and naked is nice. The amount of sports-drink on me, not so much. And then there's the sweat. And the come."

Ben laughed and stumbled in the direction of the bathroom. "You're nuts."

"No, just disgusting." Tim followed along, very

closely. "Where's Tippy? I don't want to trip on her when I get out of the shower."

"She's napping on the couch." At least, he hoped she was napping. He didn't want to think of her watching...

"Cool. Does she sleep there at night?" Tim went into the bathroom with him and started stripping.

"Yep. That's *her* spot." He would have started the water and stripped himself, but he was too busy watching Tim's pretty muscles slowly appear.

"Good." Tim peeled off his shorts and grinned. "I didn't want to have to fight her for the bed."

"Nah. Just me." God, the man was gorgeous. And sweaty. But mostly gorgeous.

"You, I'm not going to fight." Stinky socks were tugged off and then tighty-whiteys. "You're still dressed." Tim wasn't. Not at all.

"Yep. You're not." Which was stupid to say out loud, but he'd just come hard -- down Tim's throat at that -- and there was a gorgeous, naked man standing in his bathroom. He should be forgiven for being a little distracted.

Tim's grin grew and he stepped forward, crowding into Ben's personal space. "I'm not. I kind of like being naked around you." He reached out and slid his hands under Ben's shirt. "I'd like more being naked *with* you."

"Yeah, okay." He pushed into Tim's touch, his cock perking right back up. Nothing for so long, and now his body wanted a two-fer. His head did, too; he thought that would be a fine idea.

Tim seemed to be on the same wavelength. He didn't waste time getting Ben's shirt off, or helping to ease Ben's shorts down. Plus, Tim's cock was poking him in the thigh, so that was a pretty good sign, too.

Ben finally snapped out of it and started helping, and then they were both naked and kissing.

"Water," Tim mumbled into the kiss. "Hot water." He had his hands buried in Ben's hair and didn't show any inclination of letting him go.

"Water," Ben repeated, pushing against Tim's body, sliding against the sweat-slicked skin.

Tim kissed him even deeper, one hand tugging a little too hard at his hair for a moment. "Oh, God. Shower." Tim finally broke away and climbed in the tub. "Wash my back for me? For real?"

"Yeah. Whatever you want." He leaned over and turned on the water, getting it all going before stepping in and pulling the curtain, closing them in a warm, wet space.

"I want lots of things." Tim reached for him, washing water over them both. "At the moment I'm a little fixated, though."

"Yeah, you needed the shower pretty badly." He knew damn well that wasn't what Tim meant, but he couldn't help teasing, now that he thought they were past the curse.

Tim blinked at him for a moment and then laughed. "I was thinking more about your cock and various parts of me." His hand cupped Ben's balls gently. "If you tease, I will, too," he said, still grinning.

"Your teasing involves touching," Ben pointed out smugly.

"Yup." Tim's smiled grew a little wicked and his fingers edged back behind Ben's balls. "It does. Gonna wash my back?" Warm, wet fingers pushed up and rubbed.

He groaned, spreading his legs for Tim. "Not if it means you're going to stop doing that."

Tim rubbed again, his fingers making small circles and nudging at his gland. "I'm not going to stop if you keep making those sounds."

"Then don't stop." He sure as hell wasn't going to do

anything to discourage the touches.

"Lean back." Tim urged him to lean on the wall and find his balance, legs slightly spread. Then Tim kissed him again, the shower water hitting them both. With one hand, Tim kept rubbing and caressing, his fingers occasionally edging back to tease around his hole. With the other, Tim seemed to touch him everywhere else between kisses.

Ben touched back, fingers finding Tim's nipples and rubbing them, flicking across them.

"I knew you'd be like this," Tim whispered in his ear. His fingers traced up Ben's cock and swept over the head. "After you got going, anyway." The hand between Ben's legs shifted, parting his ass cheeks a little.

"Like what?" He wasn't being too desperate, was he? It just felt so good, and they'd been dancing around it so long.

"Hot." Tim licked his earlobe. "Eager. Fun. Did I mention hot?" Ben could feel Tim's prick, hard and heavy, resting along his thigh as Tim got as close as he could. "So sexy." Tim's voice washed over him like the water as one fingertip flicked barely in and out of Ben's body.

"Oh, fuck. See, this is why I don't like doing it in the shower." They needed to get horizontal. "You clean enough?"

Tim nodded, but it took him a moment to ease away. His pupils had dilated again, and he was looking at Ben with frank need on his face. "Bed now?" He stepped directly under the spray and dragged his hand over his chest, getting rid of the last of the sweat.

"Yeah." Ben reached out to slide his hand from Tim's throat, all the way down to cup the hard cock. "I have condoms." He'd nearly thrown them out, thinking the curse was because he was overeager.

Luckily, he hadn't.

"Thank God. Mine are all the way at my house." Tim

shuddered and turned off the water. "I need you, Ben. You're under my skin."

"Come on, then. You can have me." He grabbed Tim's hand and tugged him out of the shower.

They were going to get to do this.

Maybe they could come back and do it again after the barbecue -- they had a lot of time to make up for.

Chapter Thirteen

Tim dried off as best he could, considering his hands were shaking. He'd had a bit of guilt about just going off like a rocket two steps inside the door, but now... Now he'd be able to do this and make it good. Yay them for planning.

He waited until Ben was dry-ish, as well, before leaving the bathroom. "I forgot to bring my bag up from the car," he said, looking at the pile of clothes on the floor. "Does Tippy fetch?" He didn't care, not about Tippy and not about clothes; he was trying not to babble about how beautiful Ben was. God, and the guy had zero idea, too.

"You need your bag? Now? I've got lube, too..."

Tim let it go, it would take too long to explain. "Perfect." He put a hand on the small of Ben's back and tried very hard not to shove him onto the bed. "Perfect." Oh, nice bed. Big bed. Naked Ben on a bed. Tim made himself breathe. "I've been looking forward to this."

Ben nodded and popped up to go to his dresser, pulling a box of condoms and a tube of lube out of one of the drawers. They got tossed on the bed and then Ben followed, bouncing a little. "Come on."

Tim's cock lifted eagerly and he grinned. "You don't have to ask twice." Quickly, he tore open the box and got a condom from the strip. "How do you like it?"

"I want to see you, Tim."

Tim flashed him a quick smile. "Personal favorite." A moment later, rubber on, he was back to kissing Ben and wondering if, just maybe, he'd be able to freeze time if he tried hard enough. Ben kissed like it was the best thing in the world, and Tim had to appreciate that.

Ben's hands slid over his chest, fingers rubbing across his nipples. With a groan, not quite able to make himself tell Ben to stop, Tim reached for the lube. Every flick was making his cock twitch, and he just wanted in. They'd waited so long. Far, far too long, long enough that he'd pretty much given up. He probably would have, if Ben hadn't been at the race.

"I'm glad you came to the race," he whispered, watching Ben's eyes and he slipped wet fingers slowly into him.

Ben's eyes went wide, his legs spreading for him. "Uh-huh. Race." Ben nodded.

"Race." Tim nodded his encouragement and fingered Ben a bit. "It was a good race. We won."

"Yeah. Good job." Ben bucked, moved into his fingers. "Why are we talking about the race?"

"So I don't shove my way into your ass and go off like a bottle rocket," Tim confessed.

"Oh." Ben giggled and stroked his belly, groaning a little as he traced the muscles.

Tim quivered and made himself concentrate as he opened Ben up. He had a feeling things would be energetic, and he didn't want to have Ben walking funny at the barbecue. "Ready?" He lined up and pulled Ben's legs over his own thighs. "Feel free to yell a lot."

Ben laughed, the sound turning into a moan as Tim

started to push in.

Tight. Oh, man, was he tight. Tight and smooth and hot, and Tim was suddenly *very* glad he'd gotten off at the door since this was way better than he'd imagined. He'd imagined it a lot, too, night after night with his hand around his cock. But not like this.

Tim pushed in until he was deeply buried and paused, just to catch his breath. He hadn't even noticed he'd been holding it. Ben wasn't holding his breath, oh no. Ben was panting, giving little moans as he shifted, hands holding onto Tim.

"Ben. God." Tim pulled back a little, the drag around his cock making him want to plunge right back in again, to fuck him fast and hard.

Ben's heels dug into the backs of his thighs, tugging him closer. "I won't break."

Permission given, Tim leaned over and braced his arms, his hips driving him in with a slap. Groaning, he did it again.

"Yeah. Oh, yeah." Ben's hand wrapped around his neck, tugging him down for a kiss.

Tim shoved his tongue into Ben's mouth and then kissed him like a normal person. He hoped. His concentration was mostly on his cock, on the slip and slide and grind of fucking Ben steadily and keeping the sounds coming. The creak of the bed and the sounds of their bodies and the way they both gasped a bit each time he pushed in.

Ben moved beneath him, meeting each thrust and stealing his breath with kisses. Tim's hand grabbed at the bed covers and held on for leverage, something he hadn't done in a long while, and he leaned back on his heels as they moved. He was working up a sweat again. The angle was better this way, his cock felt huge, but he couldn't kiss Ben. That was just wrong.

Ben's mouth was open, sweet gasps and moans coming

out of him. "More. God. Tim. Tim."

Tim started to pant, his hips rocking, steadily battering away at Ben's ass. He would never have guessed that Ben would be so eager and ready -- and he wasn't about to complain. With a grunt he slammed in yet again and gathered Ben's cock in his fist, stroking hard.

"Fuck. Fuck." Ben squeezed around his cock, body going tight.

"Yes. Yes." Tim's words blended with Ben's, their voices merging and melding as Ben bucked under him. Tim's orgasm raced down his spine, and he held onto his control with iron will. "Come on, baby. Show me."

"Tim!" Ben bucked wildly beneath him and heat sprayed up between them.

"*Fuck*!" Tim watched and felt, his whole body flexing as he worked his cock into Ben's tighter-than-tight ass, riding his orgasm. The smell rose up, thick and pungent, and Tim growled as he fucked Ben furiously, reaching for his turn. "Yes, yes, yes," he chanted, pleasure pulsing through him, bright and sparkling, as he pumped into the condom.

"God. Tim." Ben tugged him down and took a kiss, long and hard.

Tim tried to talk, but the noises weren't really words. He kissed Ben, though, happily and frequently, and kept kissing him even as he pulled out and took care of the necessary chore of tossing the tissue-wrapped-rubber into the trash. When his breath started to come to him, he smiled and fell back on the bed. "Almost made the wait worthwhile."

"Almost." Ben chuckled and tugged him close, wrapping around him. "The curse is broken now -- no more waiting."

"Thank God." Tim kissed him again, not sure he'd ever get enough of that. One hand spanned the small of

Ben's back and kept him close. "If I get too touchy at the barbecue, either kick me or drag me off to the bathroom for a fast one."

"Are you out at work?" Ben's fingers slid in little circles in the small of his back.

"Sort of." Tim nodded. "Most of them know, but it's not like I drag people around and say, 'Hey, this is Ben, he's my gay lover,' you know?"

"I just want to know if I need to watch what I say, you know?"

Tim nuzzled Ben's jaw. "Nope. If *you* wanna drag me around and introduce yourself as my gay lover, that's cool. Boyfriend will do, though."

"Hey it's your barbecue and your friends -- you'll be doing the introducing, bub."

"Just so we're clear on the important part."

"Which was... drag you to the bathroom when I'm too horny to wait any longer?"

Tim grinned. "Yeah, that." He was kinda hoping that would happen sometime, if not at this particular barbecue.

"I'm pretty clear on that part." Ben stretched and glanced over at the clock. "When are we supposed to be at this barbecue of yours?"

"About now." Tim stretched, too, and admired Ben's stretch. "We need to clean up again. Also, Tippy needs to go get my clean clothes from my car."

Ben laughed and sat up, giving his ass a pat. "I'll get dressed and go get your bag. Tippy's bellhop days are long gone. Well, to be honest, she never was good at fetching anything other than a tennis ball."

"Heh, I bet." Tim propped himself up so he could get a better view of Ben. "I would have brought it up myself, but I was kinda worked up."

"You *forgot* because your mind was in your pants."

"That's what I said." Tim leered at him and winked. "You're amazing. Just so you know. I want to be on record as thinking you're the hottest thing on legs in this whole province. Likely, the country." He grinned to himself, waiting for the denial.

Ben laughed, shaking his head. "You're just saying that because you just got laid."

"Nah, if that was why, I'd only say it *before*." Pleased with his logic, Tim went back to leering while Ben found clothes.

"Am I good with jeans and a T-shirt? I mean 'barbecue' sounds pretty informal." A pair of boxers slid up over Ben's ass.

"Oh, yeah. For sure. It's steak and salad and beer, music in the backyard. We could even take a cab over, if we want to have a few."

"Yeah? And then you could come back here, spend the night..." Ben gave him a half-shy smile, a little color on his cheeks. "I mean I have the night off, no on-call or anything, and I make a mean omelet..."

"I'm sold. You know I'll pretty much not say no, right? I'm a sure bet. Also, easy. And, if it wasn't clear, really kinda into you." Tim reached out, trying to snag Ben for another kiss before he had to get up and get clean.

"Yeah, that's one of the things I like best about you." Grinning, Ben allowed himself to get reeled in, mouth eager on his.

Tim kissed him thoroughly, amused and pleased with how playful Ben could be. It wasn't getting them to the party, however. "I need to wash."

"Yeah, and I ought to get your clothes for you. It would probably be bad form for a police officer to have to arrest himself for indecent exposure." Ben smirked and scooted away.

"Plus, the handcuffs hurt like a son of a bitch."

"Damn, and here I was hoping we could play with them." Ben winked and hightailed it out of the bedroom. Tim could hear his chuckles until the front door closed on them.

After a shocked moment, Tim got up and said to the empty room, "I suppose I could be careful with them." Then he blinked and went to wash up. He had a party to get to and a boyfriend to introduce around. The curse was clearly lifted, so he could relax a little. Things were going fine.

Chapter Fourteen

So, how late are we for this shindig?" Ben asked as the car pulled up into a spot along the street.

"Not that late. Maybe late enough to catch some flack -- you left in a rush, and I probably left before some of them." Tim glanced over at him and grinned. "Maybe no one will notice anyway. Hungry?"

"I'm starving, actually. You have to be *really* hungry." All that running and then the exercise they'd indulged in. Finally. Ben could feel his grin spreading his cheeks. He probably looked like a goof. He didn't really care.

"Uh-huh. I could eat." Tim was looking at him pretty much the same way he had been since the end of the race. "And I wouldn't mind some food, either."

It was on the tip of his tongue to ask if they really had to go to this thing, but Ben figured if Tim could have gotten out of it, they would still be back at his place, making like bunnies. So he got out of the car before he could do anything he couldn't back away from.

Tim came around the car and took his hand. "Just cops and their people. No big deal, okay? We'll have a few burgers, maybe a steak. We'll be done in a few hours."

"Sounds good. And I want to meet your friends and co-workers."

"Yeah?" Tim's smile lit up. "Cool. Come on."

Tim led him up the drive and around to the backyard, where about twenty people mingled. Some were on the deck, others were on chairs under a tree. There was music, laughter, and when Tim waved, they all yelled hellos and congratulations.

Ben picked out Tim's fellow runners right away -- he'd been watching them run the race after all -- and he recognized a few fellow supporters. He hadn't been introduced to anyone, but there'd been a feeling of camaraderie during the race that seemed to be spilling over to the barbeque.

Tim looked around and grinned. "Want a beer? We gotta do the rounds and tell people who you are, and soon. Look at the ladies by the swing -- they're already whispering."

"You think they're putting two and two together?" Well, if Tim was out, then duh.

"Oh, yeah." Tim glanced at him real fast. "Is that a problem?"

"If it was a problem I wouldn't have come, but you know I'm out." He nudged Tim's shoulder. "Come on, let's get this done so I can just relax and have a good time, because I know your friends all like me."

"They're gonna love you." Tim grinned at him again and headed for the beer cooler. "Hey, Gus. This is my boyfriend, Ben. Ben, Gus. He works about four desks away from me."

Gus, to his credit, only blinked once before offering his hand. "Hey, Ben. I think I know you from somewhere?" His brow furrowed.

Ben shook Gus' hand. "Pleased to meet you. I was at the race earlier today."

"Yeah, I saw you there. That's not it. But you did a hell of a lot of cheering that suddenly makes sense." He laughed and whacked Tim on the arm hard enough to make Tim wince. "Go eat. You earned it."

"Uh-huh." Tim rubbed his arm and grabbed two bottles of beer. "Ben's a vet. You have a cat."

"Right!" Gus looked relieved. "But I let my wife take her in. Right, the vet."

"What's your cat's name?" Ben had to admit it, he could usually remember the animals, even if he'd only treated them the once.

Gus looked disgusted and slightly embarrassed. "Miss Glitter. My daughter was five when we got the cat."

Tim laughed and pressed one of the bottles into Ben's hand.

Ben chuckled. "White Persian mix, right?"

"And not a bit of glitter to be seen." Gus rolled his eyes. "But she's at least a nice cat and loves to be brushed. Thank God."

"She was a sweetie. Not all cats are well-behaved at the vet, but she seemed to take it all in stride." He raised his beer bottle in Gus' direction. "It was nice to meet you."

"You, too." Gus nodded, and almost dashed across the yard to where a few people were setting up for a game of horseshoes.

"There." Tim looked happy enough. "That should make sure everyone knows. Gus is a huge gossip."

That had Ben laughing, nearly snorting beer out of his nose, in fact. "Make sure I'm not drinking the next time you say something like that."

"What, about Gus being a gossip? Check it out." Tim pointed, laughing as well. "I'm going to grab us some food. Burger or steak?"

"Burgers are easier to eat at this kind of thing. I like

onions and relish on mine. Should I snag us a couple of seats by the swings over there?"

"Perfect." Tim passed him his beer bottle. "I'll be right over." Tim's fingers danced over Ben's wrist for a moment, and then Tim headed to the grill, already talking to the big man standing there wearing a red striped apron.

Ben made his way over to where there were a few vacant chairs, offering smiles to anyone who made eye contact with him. It was always somewhat awkward being at a party where you didn't know anyone, but he dealt with new people all the time as a vet, so he just put on his game face.

Tim was chatting animatedly with a few people, waiting for the food and looking over every few moments. It was kind of cute, really.

"Hi, I'm Heather." One of the runners from the race sat down next to him. "And you're Ben and he went and left you alone."

Ben chuckled and held out his hand to shake hers. "I am and he did. It's nice to meet you."

"He's a lot happier right now than he has been for a while." She tucked her legs up underneath her and looked over at Tim. "He's been a *bear*. Cranky and bitchy and just impossible."

Ben was not going to blush because Tim had been cranky at work during their "cursed" spell. He *wasn't*. He took a sip of his beer.

Heather grinned at him. "He's all mellow and cute now. Thanks."

He was definitely blushing now. "Um... you're welcome?"

"Can you do it to him again on Tuesday? I have to ride with him Wednesday morning." She was giggling now.

"I..." Oh, God. Were they all going to tease him this

hard? He chuckled and shook his head. "How much is it worth to you?"

"Oh man, a *lot*." She laughed and patted him on the arm. "I'll stop now. But seriously -- he's been just foul. I hope his good mood keeps up."

"Yeah, me too." Because he so didn't want it to be another couple months before they managed to do it again. He looked over toward Tim, hoping his burger was on its way.

Tim was looking back -- again -- and smiling. The guy in the apron had to wave a hand in front of Tim's face to get his attention.

Ben shook his head and turned back to Heather. "So, you ride with Tim sometimes?"

"Yeah, sometimes. We don't really have assigned partners, but Tim and I like to ride together when we need to double up. He's a nice guy, and he doesn't bitch that I can outrun him."

Tim was busy piling onions and pickles on burgers, between waving his hands around as he talked and laughed with his friends.

"You can? I thought he was the fastest guy on the team..." He was going to have to tease Tim about that if it was true.

"Who the hell told you that?" She laughed and shook her head. "He's speedy, but he's distance and endurance. I can take him on a sprint any day."

Oh, he was so going to needle Tim. And the longer he got left here on his own while Tim chatted up the man at the grill, the longer he was going to tease.

"Tim told me that, actually." No reason he had to be the only one with ammunition for teasing.

"That lying son of a bitch!" Heather grinned widely. "I bet he told you all kinds of other bullshit, too. He's a cop and a man, honey -- only believe about half of what he tells you. Although, if Tim's talking about how much he works out, he's probably telling the truth."

"He does seem rather obsessed with the working out thing. Is that another cop thing?"

"No, that's a vain, pretty man thing." She rolled her eyes and got up. "In his case, it really kind of works, don't you think?"

"What does?" Tim bumped her out of the way and stole her chair, passing Ben a plate loaded up with chips and burger.

He smirked. "The vain, pretty man thing."

"I'm pretty?"

"Oh, for God's sake." Heather stole some of Tim's chips. "You're pretty. And human again, thanks to Ben."

Tim looked at Ben. "What have you been telling this horrible woman?"

Oh, God. "Nothing, I swear. She guessed." He grabbed his burger and took a huge mouthful so he wouldn't have to say anything else.

"She's a *cop*, of course she guessed." Tim laughed and sat back. "Go away, Heather. I'm not going to give you details, ever."

"You'd better not," Ben mumbled around his mouthful. "And, yes, you're pretty. Well. Studly, really."

"I won't." Tim leaned closer, one hand curled around his burger. He looked around for a moment and winked. "She's fun." Then his voice dropped low. "You're pretty, too. And studly. And you get me really hot."

Ben figured he was going to have to accept the fact that his cheeks were going to be permanently red.

"Eat up," Tim said around a mouthful of burger. "We can play horseshoes for a bit."

He munched on his burger, deliberately staying focused on the food and not looking to see if everyone was checking them out. It was easier being the center of gossip if you weren't actually around to see it going on.

"They'll be nice," Tim assured him. "I think Heather is probably the crudest of the bunch, and you did okay with her. Oh, but some of the wives can be nosy. Ask them about their kids if you want to deflect attention, that'll get them yammering for an hour and they'll think you're the nicest thing ever."

"Oh, I can do that. I suppose it's a kind of initiation thing, too. Ribbing the new guy."

"Uh-huh. Just like that. It's a compliment, really. And the fact that I've never actually brought anyone to these things has them all kinds of stirred up." Tim said it really casually, like it was no big deal.

Ben's eyebrows went up. "Really? No one to anything, ever?" It might not have been a big deal to Tim, but it was to Ben. It made him feel really good to hear that.

Tim blushed, his cheeks going pink. "No one. Not ever. You're... well, you're special."

He reached out and touched Tim's thigh. "Thanks."

"Thanks for coming. And not running away from Heather. I have to drive with her this week." Tim tangled their fingers together for a moment.

"Yeah, so she said. She also thanked me for putting you in a better mood and told me you were not the fastest runner on the team."

"Heather lies."

"You're saying you *are* the fastest? For real, or just in your mind?" He couldn't help teasing. "Should I take a poll?"

"No!" Tim grinned at him and shook his head. "No polls. And Heather *does* lie, all the time. Just stating a fact."

"Ah, but not about this, obviously." He poked Tim in the ribs. "You lie, too, then."

"I do not!" Tim tossed his plate on the grass and

wiggled away from Ben's finger, laughing. "I beat her at anything over a hundred meters!"

"Yeah, but the hundred meters is what counts -- that's who they call the fastest man in the world at the Olympics."

"Bet I could beat you. Bet I could beat Tippy!"

"A snail could beat, Tippy, man. That's pretty sad if you're trying to make points against a geriatric dog." God, this was fun.

Tim snorted. "I bet you, too. Bet you a favor of your choice that I can beat you in a hundred meters."

"But that's a sucker bet because I *know* you can beat me. And my dog."

"So do I win?" Tim's grin turned into a leer. "Favor of my choice?"

"I'm not betting with you. But you can still have a favor of your choice." Anything Tim wanted.

Tim gave him a long look. "Want to skip the horseshoes? Make up our own games?"

"Your friends won't think it rude?" They'd barely put in an appearance.

"My friends will know why we left, which is probably worse than them thinking we're rude." Tim rolled his eyes. "One game of horseshoes. Another burger. Then we're so out of here."

"Oh, yeah, please. I mean, they're going to think it anyway, but I'd rather not confirm it, you know?" He shook himself. "I don't want to think of them thinking of us... you know."

Tim snickered. "Most of them would rather poke out their eyes than think about it. The rest are jealous."

"Come on, let me beat you at horseshoes. And then you can owe me a sexual favor of *my* choice."

"Are you asking me to take a dive?" Tim hauled him to his feet. "I'd do anything you ask, anyway."

"Oh, you won't have to take a dive. I'm going to beat you fair and square." After all, he was a vet, and it was *horse*shoes.

"We'll see." Tim took his hand and dragged him off to the pitch. "They're not actually on a horse, you know."

"Thank God for that. There's no way I could lift a horse, let alone throw it."

Tim laughed hard, hard enough that people started looking and smiling. He was still laughing when he tugged Ben to where the others were standing. "This is Ben," he said, wiping his eyes. "He's funny as hell, and he's gonna win."

"Oh, man, no pressure there." He rolled his eyes and shook hands with the others. "I do know how to play, though."

"Good, Tim forgets there's rules." An older guy with salt and pepper hair stuck out his hand. "I'm Steve, that's Kimball and Rob."

"I do not," Tim said indignantly. "You lot cheat."

"Man, for a bunch of cops, you guys sure do lie and cheat a lot."

"Now you're catching on." Tim beamed at him and picked up the horseshoes. "Okay, let's do this. I've got ten bucks that says Ben wins."

"You're going to put money on me with your friends, eh? What if *I* lie, too?" He liked that Tim believed in him, though. He liked that the faith was right there.

"Then I'm out ten bucks and you owe me." Tim shrugged and winked at him. "I win, either way. But you'll win."

Steve made retching noises and begged someone to bring him beer.

Ben laughed and grabbed his horseshoes. "Watch and learn."

"Go for it, baby." Tim stepped back and shoved Steve.

Hard. "Behave now, or I'll sic Heather on you."

Ben only got close with his first shoe, but the other three hit the post, the metal on metal sound ringing out. Tim just freaking beamed at him, and the others looked pretty impressed.

"Do it again," Rob said, lifting his chin and laughing. "Prove it's not a fluke."

Tim whacked him on the arm. Hard.

"It's not a fluke." Ben shot another set, managing to get all of these, grinning as Tim cheered. "See?"

Rob, Steve and Kimball all looked at Tim in disgust. "There'll be no living with him now," Steve muttered. "But we'll keep the ringer and drag him to the next event. Maybe we can beat the FD again."

Ben laughed. "I'm afraid it's my one and only talent in the sports arena."

"We'll take it. If you can beat the FD at anything, we'll take it."

Tim laughed and handed the horseshoes to Rob. "Here you go. Our work here is done, unless you really want Ben to humiliate you further?"

"It was nice to meet you guys." Ben shook hands with everyone again. "I'm not going to get quizzed on names later, am I? I really am better with animals."

"Just call Rob 'Skippy', Steve 'Butch' and Kimball 'Killer'," Tim suggested. And then Tim ran, chased by Rob.

"I don't know how you guys still have the energy to run..."

"Tim doesn't have an off button, and Rob's just as bad," Steve said with a roll of his eyes. "Work hard, play harder. You'll get used to it."

"Yeah, I hope so." He'd like to have all the time in the world to get used to it.

"If you don't, just yell at him. Works for my wife."

Steve blushed bright red. "Not that I'm saying you're the girl, mind. I mean. Oh, fuck."

Ben and Kimball both laughed. "I'm telling Tim you said he was the girl."

"Jesus Christ, I need a beer." Still red, Steve wandered off, looking utterly embarrassed.

"Oh, yeah. Keeping you." Kimball beamed at him. "You might want to go collect Tim before he hurts himself, though."

Oh, Ben didn't want Tim wearing himself out. That was his job. He headed across the yard to cut Tim off mid-chase.

"Oh, hey." Tim pulled up short, letting Rob escape. He was flushed and panting a bit, but the run around the house didn't seem to have caused him any harm. "All done?"

"Yeah. In fact, I have Kimball and Steve's blessing to take you home. I think. But then Steve also said you were the girl, so..."

Tim blinked at him and his mouth fell open. "He what?"

"Well, technically, he said he wasn't calling me the girl..."

"I really don't think I want to know what you were talking about. Can we go to my place now?" He took Ben's hand and started urging him to the car.

"We need to stop by my place and let Tippy out first."

"Oh, right. Really? It's only been a couple of hours. Okay, we'll skip my place. I'm easy."

"Um... well, I thought you were inviting me to stay the night. If I got it wrong, though..."

Tim stopped walking and looked at him, his eyes a little wide and a lot dark. "Yeah? You would? I didn't think you'd leave Tippy overnight. You had mentioned me staying and then omelets. But if you come to my place for the night, I promise you waffles for breakfast."

"Tippy'll be okay if I check in on her now and ask Stacey to take her out in the morning." He gave Tim a wry grin. "If we stay at your place, I can't accidently get called in."

"Right, then. We're going to my place. Let's go let Tippy out and get your toothbrush." He started moving again, rushing Ben to the car.

Ben laughed, but he kind of knew how Tim felt. Eager and ready, and just a little bit worried that if they dawdled, something would come up and interrupt them.

Not this time, though. The curse was lifted now.

Chapter Fifteen

Tim let them into his apartment and flicked on the lights in the kitchen as he walked down the hall. There was a lamp in the living room, but he'd forgotten to leave it on, of course. At least he didn't trip as he led Ben around. It wasn't dark outside yet, but his apartment didn't get any afternoon light at all.

"So, that wasn't too bad, was it?" he asked Ben, hoping that his friends hadn't actually traumatized him. "They can be a bit... uh, loud."

"And in your face. But that's okay, that one guy said you were the girl, so I think I survived okay."

Tim really was going to have to deal with that. Man, some people's children. He rolled his eyes and laughed, then tugged Ben onto the couch with him. "Yeah, I'm the girl. You should bring me flowers and stuff. Want to watch a movie?"

"Sure, I'll even let you choose which one as long as it's not a girly movie." Oh, he could see Ben was planning on having fun with this.

"*Terms of Endearment.* Or maybe *When Harry Met Sally.* Oh, I know, *Bridges of Madison County.*" Tim

137

nuzzled his way into the crook of Ben's neck. "Or you could just fuck me over the couch. Is that girly?"

"Not if you've got a penis it's not." Ben's mouth met his, the kiss eager and hard, ready.

Tim kissed him back just as hard. He absolutely had a penis, and he rubbed it on Ben's thigh to make sure they both were well aware of the fact. He had one, and he really, really wanted to get it out of his clothes. Then he wanted Ben's out of *his* clothes, and after that, they'd just see what they came up with.

"Oh, God. I can't believe we're getting to do this again. Did you unplug your phone?" Ben's hands moved on him, randomly touching.

Tim reached one hand over to the table by the couch and pawed around until he found the phone. Then he pulled, really hard. "Yeah, it's taken care of." The phone hit the floor with a clatter and Tim started working on Ben's clothes. "Want you."

Ben laughed, but also helped with the clothes, so that was okay. There were maybe going to be a few rips and missing buttons here and there. That was okay, too.

"God. You smell good." Tim kissed his way across Ben's chest, his fingers busy with the final task of shoving Ben's shorts down. "Like sex and grass and summer." He felt good, too, hot and hard in Tim's hand.

"Sweet-talker." Ben pushed into his hands and into his mouth, moaning softly.

"It's true." Tim licked one of Ben's nipples and bit it lightly. His hand was curled around Ben's cock, not really stroking him hard -- yet -- but holding onto him and tracing the soft skin. "I have to go get some stuff from the bedroom."

Groaning, Ben held onto him. "No, stay."

Tim ground his cock against Ben's thigh. "Want you in me. That means I need to get stuff." But he stayed where he was and kissed Ben again, unable to resist.

"Shit, don't say stuff like that -- you're going to make me shoot."

"Not yet." Tim sucked a light mark on Ben's neck. "Not until you're in my ass."

Ben made a strangled noise. "You'd better go get that stuff."

Tim rolled to his feet and walked to his room, his cock leading the way. He didn't waste any time at all getting the lube and a strip of condoms; he just sprawled across the bed and got them, then bounded to his feet and hurried back. "Oh, good. You're still here." Grinning, he popped the top on the lube.

"Still here, still naked, still horny as hell."

"Me, too." Tim climbed onto Ben's lap, straddling his hips. "You're amazing. Wanna fuck?"

"I do. Over and over again. And then some more." Ben slipped a hand behind Tim's head and tugged him down for a kiss.

"Oh, lucky me," Tim whispered just as their mouths met. "Like this?" He plunged his tongue into Ben's mouth and shifted his hips so he could rub along Ben's erection.

Ben sucked hard on his tongue, body bowing, nearly bucking him off. "Shit, Tim. Condom. Now."

Tim had to lean back and find them; he hadn't even noticed when they'd dropped. Breathing heavily, he got one of the foil packets open and handed Ben the lube. "Let's go." He lifted up onto his knees and smoothed the rubber down over Ben, trying not to hurry too much, trying not to be desperate, even though he was.

Ben slicked up his fingers -- and his arm and his stomach before he was done -- and pushed two finger into Tim. There was no finesse, but that was okay, he didn't need finesse, not as hot as he was for it.

"God, yes." Tim let his eyes close as he took Ben's

fingers. He could feel his own cock start to leak as Ben opened him up, and part of him wanted to just go like that, riding Ben's fingers until he shot. Most of him, however, really wanted to feel Ben's prick filling him up, so he made himself open his eyes and meet Ben's gaze. "In me," he said. He thought he might sound like he was pleading.

"That enough?" Ben was already pulling out his fingers, though.

"Yeah, yeah. Perfect." He had no idea. He didn't care. He just wanted to sink down on Ben's cock and ride him hard. "God, hurry."

Ben lined his prick up, bumping his balls first, but then, oh fuck, then finding his hole and just pushing in like they both needed.

"Yes!" Tim's back arched as he let himself meet Ben's thrust. The stretch was nice and sharp, an added edge. Now all he had to do was keep himself from coming long enough to enjoy it.

"God. Fuck." Ben grabbed hold of his hips, fingers curling around them tight enough to leave bruises. Movement followed, Ben humping up into him.

Bracing himself with his hands on the back of the couch, Tim took it and met it, lifting himself up by the strength of his thighs and then slamming back down. Within moments they'd found a fast and hard rhythm; when Ben pegged his gland, though, Tim lost it.

"Fuck! Yes!" Tim stopped moving and hoped to hell that Ben would do it again and again.

Ben did, moaning and groaning and going to town. Tim's eyes would have crossed if they'd been open. As it was, though, he just held onto the back of the couch and let waves of pleasure roll over him in faster and faster rushes, until he wasn't able to take it any longer. Then he let go of the couch, grabbed his cock, and stroked once.

"Ben!" He yelled the name as he started to shoot, and if his neighbors had any doubt over Ben's identity before, they didn't any longer.

"Tim!" His own name echoed in the room, Ben jerking and filling the condom.

At least they knew their own names. Tim grinned foolishly as his cock gave one last leap and throb, then buried his head in Ben's neck. "God damn. That was good." He was sweating and panting and they were both getting sticky with come. It could hardly have been better.

Ben made an indistinct noise and patted his back. "I'm never moving again."

"Uh-huh. Totally with you." Tim kept on panting and enjoying the tingles that were still settled in his spine. "Until, of course, it's time to go to bed and do it again."

"Yeah. Gonna pass out here for now, though." Ben gave him a goofy grin, eyes at half-mast.

With a long groan, Tim lifted himself enough to let Ben slip away from him. "Gotta clean up. At least a bit." Luckily there were tissues handy, and clean-up was taken care of with ease. "Couldn't fuck like this on your couch. Tippy would be pissed." Tim curled around Ben and reached for the remote.

"Ew. Dog-watching is not conducive to love-making."

"Exactly. So, we keep it to the bed and shower at your place. My place can be couch sex and workout room. And bed. Oh, and kitchen." Tim grinned, warming to his topic as he flipped through channels and tried to find a movie on TV.

Laughing, Ben snuggled in. "You got a blanket handy?"

Tim nodded and set the remote down, then yanked the blanket out from under their butts. "One blanket, not even sticky. But we really should make it to the bed before we fall asleep for the night."

"Yeah, I just don't want to sit here butt-naked without at least a cover."

"I don't mind." Tim covered them and snuggled up, one hand going right to cup Ben's soft cock. "I won't let anyone see you," he teased.

"Looks like you're going to keep me warm, too." Ben's arm went around him, tugging him a little closer. "Oh, hey, that was one of the Indiana Jones movies -- go back."

Tim turned the channel back and settled in. He'd had an amazing day, and while he knew that they all couldn't be that good -- race winning, barbecues with good people, amazing sex and a great movie on TV -- he had hopes that more of them would end with Ben in his arms as the sun went down.

That would make any day a winner, no matter what.

Chapter Sixteen

Ben handed Bingo's leash to Jimmy, the boy clutching it to his chest as the little hound and beagle mix wagged his tail like crazy and barked for Jimmy's attention.

"So, he's okay, Dr. Sauvigon ? He's not gonna die?"

Shaking his head, Ben ruffled Jimmy's hair. "He's just fine. He pooped that piece of Lego out like a pro. Oh, here." Digging into his pocket, he handed over the offending Lego piece. "You need to be more careful, though, Jimmy. Next time, he might eat something that doesn't just come out as nicely as this did. Bingo could really hurt himself if he eats things he's not supposed to."

"I learned my lesson, Dr. Sauvigon. I'm gonna take real good care of Bingo, I promise."

"I'm sure you will." He watched Jimmy join his mother, the little dog's back end still wagging hard. He glanced at his watch. Almost one. "Amy, do I have time to take a lunch today?"

"Well, you *would* have time to have lunch, except a Constable Geary is here to see you."

"Oh, send him in, please."

She gave him a sniff and Ben grinned. Tim never was going to get on her good side, by the looks of it. He held the waiting room door open, scanning the chairs for his lover.

He wasn't hard to miss, getting to his feet in his full uniform, heavy belt creaking. "Thanks, Amy," Tim said, winking outrageously at her. "I'll try not to keep him long."

Ben admired the whole full-uniform cop look, grinning.

"My cop boyfriend is sexy," he told Tim, once the door was closed.

"Better than a fireman?" Tim grinned at him and took off his hat.

"Uh-huh. Because you do this." He dug his fingers into Tim's utility belt and tugged him close, bringing their mouths together.

Tim backed him up against the wall and kissed him hard, one hand cupping Ben's face. "Hey, I like this." Tim smiled at him and kissed him again, his hips making a tiny circle.

"It'd be even better in my office." It was one thing if Stacey or Amy happened upon them, quite another if it was a client.

Tim nodded and manhandled him in that direction. "And you'll be happy to know I'm not just here to get my noon kisses."

"No? Because I'm pretty happy with just the noon kisses."

"The noon kisses are kind of the personal priority, yes." Tim dragged Ben into the office and closed the door. "The work stuff can wait until after I get a few more."

"There's work stuff?" He didn't give Tim a chance to answer, though, just dove into the 'more kisses' part.

God, Tim *was* a good kisser.

Tim didn't seem to be in a hurry to get to any kind of work stuff at all. In fact, he seemed pretty determined to turn kissing into rubbing, and thrusting, and a bit of panting, too.

Ben grabbed onto Tim's ass and went with it, humping back against Tim. There were lots of hard things on Tim's belt, rubbing against him along with Tim's cock. Ben had to admit, it was sexier than he'd expected.

With a low groan, Tim seemed to push even harder, and certainly faster. "God, yes. Missed you last night," he whispered in Ben's ear. "Lock the door, let me blow you."

"Fuck." He reached back and locked the door.

"Not enough time for that." Tim was already going to his knees, not even bothering with the buttons on Ben's lab coat. He just shoved it up and got to work on Ben's belt.

Ben tried to help, his cock suddenly desperately hard. He wasn't sure how Tim managed to do that to him, but as Tim was going to take care of it, he didn't much care.

One of Tim's hands petted him through his pants, hot and heavy, but then the zipper worked and his cock pushed out, right into Tim's fist. "There we go," Tim whispered, right before he started licking.

Ben watched, wide-eyed, at the pretty sight of Tim on his knees, in his full uniform, working at Ben's prick. It didn't get much better than that.

Then Tim started undoing his own pants, one hand holding onto Ben's hip and the other fighting to get his zipper undone, in between hard rubs over the uniform and even harder sucks of Ben's cock.

"God, that's pretty. Tim." Ben's head clunked as it dropped back against the door, and he shoved his hand into his mouth to muffle his groans.

Tim made a humming noise that sounded like agreement, and took him in deeper. Ben heard the zipper finally slide, and Tim's efforts redoubled as his head bobbed, the wet sucking sounds almost masking the sound of Tim jacking off. Almost.

He watched for a few more moments, Tim's head bobbing on his prick, the edge of Tim's hand as it appeared and disappeared in rapid succession. And then he closed his eyes and just felt. The suction got tighter, then looser, and Tim seemed to take him in deeper with each stroke. When Tim let go of his hip, it was only to pet and roll Ben's balls. Then the fingers edged back a little, just as Tim's sounds took on a desperate edge.

It was Tim's noises that really pushed him over, making him jerk and cry out as he shot down Tim's throat.

He could feel Tim jerking as he swallowed, the groans turning to grunts and the smell of sex rising up fast. Tim licked him a little between panted breaths, then said, "Tissues, baby. I need tissues. Full hands."

"My desk." He sidled out from between Tim and the door and went to his desk, grabbing a couple of tissues and handing them over.

Tim was grinning broadly as he wiped his hands. "Nice. I like your office."

Snorting, Ben went and flopped in his chair. "You can come for lunch *anytime*."

"Awesome." Tim wiped his hands again and even used the sanitizer on Ben's desk, then put himself away and did up his pants. "I'll come by as often as I can."

Ben's stomach rumbled. "Did you bring any actual lunch?"

"I was going to take you around the corner to the diner, if you had time. If not, I'll bring you some as soon as we're done."

Ben glanced at his watch. "That should be fine -- they

serve pretty quickly. Especially closer to one. So I assume you're actually here with news?"

"Yeah." Tim sat in the client chair and took out his notebook. "As you thought, all of the pets that we had access to died of the same toxic substance, though some had a lot higher concentration than others. The lab thinks that was mainly due to the size of the animal and how much of it they ate. With the bodies of the pets from the last series, we were able to confirm that the poison was eaten, as opposed to injected or anything else. That makes is harder to find a suspect, since the person wouldn't actually need to be around, he could just leave the food and go."

"Damn. Have you got anyone on your radar?"

"Yes, I do. I spent a huge part of last week talking to everyone, over and over. I was lucky I could even run on the weekend, I logged so many hours walking the neighborhoods. There were all the usual neighborhood grudges, of course, but a lot of the people described the same young man being around. He turned up more and more often the closer I got to the high school, so I'm going to go talk to the school principal this afternoon."

"I hope you get him. I'd like to call the news and ask them to tell people to keep an eye on their pets and not let them eat anything they haven't given themselves. I don't want any more dead animals in my clinic."

Tim nodded. "It's a good idea. I've been spreading the word to everyone as I've been going. Come on, I'll buy you lunch. With any luck, I'll have good news for you later on today."

"That would be awesome." He picked up the phone and dialed Amy. "I'm going to be out of the office for about forty-five minutes."

She sniffed. "With him?"

"I'm not saying."

She harumphed, leaving him laughing as he hung up.

"She hates me," Tim said with a huge grin.

"Yeah, she really does. I'm still not sure what you did to her, either." He stood and stretched. "Come on, I'm *starving,* and you promised me lunch."

"And lunch you shall have." Tim picked up his hat and kissed Ben once more before putting it on. "Hopefully, they'll have a booth open, and we can play footsie."

Laughing, Ben pinched Tim's ass.

It was turning out to be a banner day.

Chapter Seventeen

There were days when nothing went right, and there were days that seemed to be blessed. Tim was having a mostly in-between day, though it was leaning to the good. There had been noon orgasms and lunch, and the high school didn't seem to be interested in making things hard for him.

In fact, the high school seemed willing to give him a list of kids and everything they'd done wrong, ever. Maybe it was time to talk to the chief again about having a cop in the school as a community liaison and a visible presence. Not a job Tim wanted for himself, but it might be something someone really wanted to tackle.

He spent an hour or so with the guidance counselor, talking about the pets and the young man people had seen. She agreed that the description might fit one or two of the students, but didn't seem to think that any of them would be doing something as aggressive as killing animals. Tim pointed out that poison wasn't really aggressive, and could therefore be twisted into something they didn't really *do*, and she reluctantly conceded to the point.

She wouldn't, however, let him talk to the students

without their parents being called in. Tim knew that she was right about that, but when one of the three senior students turned out to be truant, he went looking on his own, the boy's address in his hand.

No one was home, and the neighbors hadn't seen anyone at the house in a few days. The newspapers weren't piling up, however, so Tim planned to come back at the supper hour. In the meantime, he called Ben's office to fill him in.

Amy answered the phone. "Terry Road Veterinary Clinic."

"Hello, Amy. It's Officer Geary. Is Ben around? It's business, not social." Maybe if he said it right up front, she might thaw a bit.

"I'll put you through." He couldn't tell from her voice if she'd thawed at all.

"Thank you," he said, making sure he was smiling. Someone had told him that people could hear a smile.

"Ben Sauvigon." Ben sounded harried, maybe even grumpy.

"Hey, you. Bad day?"

"Tim. Hi. Yeah, I had another dead dog after you left."

"Christ." Tim sighed. "Okay, I'll come and pick him up. I'll be working tonight, trying to get hold of a kid and his parents."

"Oh. I was hoping we were going to be able to get together, but this is too important."

Tim nodded to himself and resisted the urge to sigh again. "It is. But if I'm done by about eight, I could come by. Is nine too late?"

"Ten's not too late if you're up for a quickie."

"I'm *always* up for a quickie, if it's what you want." Tim laughed and rolled his eyes. "I can't imagine working that late tonight unless I make an arrest. How about you expect me to come by, and if I don't, you can assume it's actually good news?"

"Okay, that sounds great. Good luck -- I hope you find this kid."

"Me, too." Tim's voice grew serious. "I really do. These things escalate. Not that pets aren't horrible, but you know what I mean. Whoever is doing this, kid or not, needs some serious help."

"Yeah, I think I pointed that out myself back when this first started." He could hear Ben's grin. "Look, I've got to go, I've got a few more patients to see. I'll tell Amy to send you right in to exam room two for the dog when you come."

"Okay. I'll see you tonight, I hope." He disconnected and looked at his phone, then back at the empty house. He really, really hoped this would go easy.

Ben gave up waiting for Tim to come have dinner at eight. He'd been hoping they could eat together, but he supposed, as Tim had said, him not being here was good news. He popped some microwave popcorn and had a large bottle of water, settling in front of something nice and mindless on the TV.

Tippy sat at her end of the couch, snoring softly.

He could admit to himself that he was waiting for Tim to show up. Every time he thought of the guy, he got a semi. He glanced at his watch and flipped channels. How come he used to be able to spend his evenings by himself and now he was antsy and unable to settle?

Okay, so he knew why. He shook his head at himself and found a comedy to watch.

He heard the car door slam before he realized he'd even heard an engine. The footsteps coming up the steps were welcome, though, heavy and solid, the same as the knock at the door. "Still up?" Tim called through the screen in the door.

"Come on in, man." He put his popcorn bowl on the coffee table and hauled himself up.

All right.

Tim came in, still in his uniform, though he was already undoing the heavy belt. "I'm so glad you're still up." He looked beat, but not exhausted.

"Me, too. I'm glad you came by." He met Tim halfway, wrapping his arms around Tim's waist and holding on.

Tim hugged him just as hard, then took a kiss. "I heard there were quickies on offer. And maybe a beer?"

"Yeah. Tell me what's new first. No, wait, I want another kiss first." He took it, hand going behind Tim's head to hold him in place. He gave Tim a proper, long, hello kiss.

Tim gave him another one, and there were cop hands suddenly on his butt.

Ben laughed. Yeah, this first. Wriggling, he rubbed his ass back into Tim's hands.

"Your place, no couch sex." Tim laughed softly and kissed him again, then started backing him into the nearest wall.

"Mmm..." His back hit the wall with a thud and he groaned. "Bed?"

"Bed sex is always good." The hands on his ass started kneading. "I had a long day. You kind of make it worth it."

"Oh." He cupped Tim's face and kissed him hard. "Thank you."

"Let me thank you when we're naked," Tim suggested with a bright smile. "Bed now? Please? Or even the shower would be good."

"Shower if you want to get clean before we hit bed.

I'll blow you." He owed Tim one. "But first, what's the news?"

"Oh, blow me in the shower?" Tim's eyes glazed over for a moment. "Uh, kid's parents came home, I talked to them, they did some searching and found him in the basement, stoned out of his gourd. They allowed me to take him to the hospital, and we all got him signed in to a secured ward until tomorrow morning, when they're all going to meet me at the station and I'll finally be able to talk to him. I don't know if it's him. I just don't, not yet. But, if nothing else, the kid's got problems and now his parents know."

"Oh, that's sad. You didn't get any gut feeling off him?" He slid his hand along Tim's abs as he spoke -- Tim had a great gut.

"Kid was flying high." Tim's abs rippled. "He was angry and stoned. He didn't strike me as a happy guy, no." Tim seemed happy, though. Hard and happy and eager.

Ben helped Tim get out of his pants, kissing the tip of that happy cock. "Come on, shower -- I'm not blowing you in the bathroom, only in the shower."

"Hot water and your mouth -- can't think of much better." Tim shed the rest of his clothes and got in the shower with flattering speed.

Ben slipped out of his sweats and joined Tim. He didn't tease -- they both wanted this. He sank to his knees and began to lick the flowing water off Tim's skin.

"Man." Tim's fingers were light on his head, lifting his hair out of the way of his ears and then tracing the corner of Ben's mouth. "I thought about this more than once today."

"About me sucking you?" He took some of Tim's pubic hair between his lips and started tugging.

"Uh-huh." Tim made a rough sound and his cock

flexed. "Yeah. Do that again. I think about it a lot."

He did it again, only further down, almost at Tim's balls. Then he took one into his mouth, sucking on it.

"Oh, fuck me, yes." Tim gasped, and his legs spread a bit. "Didn't think about this, though. Well, not every time."

He tugged a little, stretching Tim's ball sac. Then he slowly opened his mouth, letting the tension pull Tim's ball out.

Above him, Tim shuddered and moaned. "Ben. Please. More."

"Don't worry, I'm not going to stop until you're done." He nibbled on Tim's other ball and then pulled it in, his suction strong.

Tim was gasping again and his fingers were tangled in Ben's hair, tugging harder and harder. "Suck me. *God*, please."

He let Tim's ball go and got right down to business, wrapping his lips around the head and licking the slit. For a moment, it felt like Tim was going to ram right in and fuck his mouth, but he held back. Ben could feel the shake in his thighs, though, and he could hear how heavily Tim was breathing. Taste was already exploding in his mouth.

He took his time, bobbing his head slowly up and down, taking a little more each time he went down.

"Yes." Tim whispered encouragement as he leaned back on the wall of the shower, his legs bending and spreading a bit more. "That's it, yes. You look so hot."

He looked up into Tim's face. Tim was the hot one, face lost to pleasure.

Tim was looking back down, and his eyes widened as their gazes met. "Ben. Gonna go." Sure enough, Ben could feel Tim's cock swelling even harder in his mouth.

He increased his suction as much as possible, hand

going to cup Tim's balls.

When Tim came, it was with a slow surge and long series of pulses, and Tim didn't look away. He looked slightly stunned, and really lost in pleasure, but he didn't close his eyes. He was right there with Ben, the whole time.

Ben pulled off, pressing kisses all along the length of Tim's prick and rubbing his cheek against it.

Tim slowly sank down to meet him, shaking slightly from his release and looking for kisses. "Come here," he managed to say, reaching for Ben. "Let me take care of you."

"Okay." Like he was ever going to say no to that.

Tim's hand found him and started petting. "Want it hard and fast? Nice and slow?" Tim's palm slid over the crown, his fingers teasing.

Ben groaned, hips pushing, searching for friction. "Depends -- are we gonna go to bed and do it again? Or just go to bed?"

"I was thinking bed, a bit of rimming, some more sucking..." Tim's fingers went lower and cupped his balls, Tim's other hand joining in to stroke Ben's cock. "Anything you want."

"It all sounds good. Everything with you does."

He groaned. "Let's save this for bed. We're going to be running out of hot water soon."

Tim's hands coasted over him again and then let him go. "Bed." Tim nodded. "Let's go to bed, so I can do this right."

"Yeah." He stood and turned off the water, quickly grabbing them a couple of towels.

Drying took a couple of minutes, since Tim seemed intent on making sure Ben's cock was really dry, and then they tumbled through to the bedroom and onto the bed. "Roll onto your stomach," Tim said, almost shoving him around.

"Pushy, pushy." Not that he was complaining. No, not one bit. He rolled onto his stomach and pulled his knees up under him, offering his ass over.

"God, just gorgeous." Tim's hands roamed over his ass and then his tongue followed, licking each cheek. "You have the best ass ever."

"Thank you." Sometimes you just accepted what your lover told you. Especially when he was licking all over your ass. Or right over your ass, as the case may be. Tim's tongue licked right over his hole, and then did it again as Tim's hands squeezed his cheeks.

He squeezed his hole tight as a shiver went through him, and then forced himself to relax, moaning at how good it felt.

Tim licked him again and again, sometimes using the flat of his tongue and sometimes just the tip, teasing around and around his hole, then blowing cool air across it. Once in a while there would be licking *and* fingers, driving him insane. Ben started rocking back onto the touches, moaning, letting Tim know how good it was.

"That's it." Tim fingered him a little more and kept on licking, occasionally biting at the tender skin of one cheek. Then he settled in to tongue-fucking Ben's ass, one hand grasping Ben's cock and giving him a tunnel to fuck.

It was perfect, rocking between Tim's mouth and his hand, feeling the pleasure rushing over him in waves.

The hand tightened, squeezing rhythmically, and Tim began to moan. The vibrations around his hole were weird, something new, and then Tim was licking up his spine, just a little ways. "When you come," he said with a voice like gravel, "I'm gonna get my cock in you so I can feel it."

Ben shuddered. "Better make it soon," he managed to

grind out.

"Get me the rubbers." Tim dove back down and went back to tonguing him.

Whimpering, he stretched out, managing to grab one off the side table. He tossed it back, just about losing his mind. He heard the foil at the same time that Tim's tongue plunged into his ass, and it was a good thing that Tim wasn't jacking him right then, or he'd be too late.

He pushed back onto Tim's tongue. He was going crazy, it was so good. His fingers curled into the sheets, his back arching. "Hurry. Hurry."

"I am!" The tongue vanished and Tim was there, leaning right over him, his cock pressing against Ben's hole. "Come on, now, baby." His hand was tight, stroking Ben quickly.

"Fuck!" Ben lost it; his body bucked, he pushed hard through Tim's hand, and that was it. He came hard.

"Yes!" Tim shoved in, his cock like a battering ram as he fucked Ben right through his orgasm. It made everything more intense, being stretched and taken so bluntly while he was shooting -- and it didn't last long. Tim must have been right on the edge, too, because almost as soon as Ben was spent, weak and shaking, Tim was yelling again and coming hard, his prick throbbing in Ben's ass.

He collapsed as soon as Tim was done, panting, enjoying the weight on his back.

"Jesus Christ." Tim didn't even seem to be trying to hold himself up. "God. Yes." A kiss was pressed to his shoulder blade. "I needed that."

"Yeah, we go more than a day or two and I start to worry the curse is back." He chuckled, finding Tim's hand and wrapping his around it. "You're going to have to roll off soon." He wasn't suffocating yet, but he could feel it starting to creep up on him.

"I can't just attach myself?" Tim groaned and kissed

him again. "Okay, moving." He didn't, though, not for another few seconds. When he did move, it was slowly, like he was weary to his bones. "I think my brains melted."

"Yeah, I can feel them leaking all over me." As soon as Tim was settled next to him, Ben burrowed in, snuggling up against Tim, and glad they were already in bed because he wasn't going to be awake for much longer.

"Can I stay?" Tim whispered in his ear, wrapping around tight. "I'll have to leave really early."

"Yeah, stay." It felt good having someone to sleep with. It felt good having *Tim* there next to him.

"Okay, yeah." It sounded like Tim was mostly on his way to sleep already. "Thanks." The arms around him squeezed for a moment, then Tim utterly relaxed, his breathing even.

Ben smiled and let himself fall asleep, warm and happy and boneless.

Chapter Eighteen

Tim surprised himself by waking up as early had he'd hoped, even without his alarm. He had a moment of confusion when he realized the light was all wrong and he wasn't alone, but seeing Ben next to him brought it all back, fast. The resulting smile made him start the day right.

He went back to his own apartment to shower and dress in a clean uniform, and went right to work. He had a family to talk to, and hopefully he'd get somewhere with the poisoning case.

When he got to the station, he found an empty interview room and took over, placing his files and a nice, huge cup of coffee on the table. He was a little early, but that was okay; better than being late and leaving the family and the boy to get increasingly upset.

The family arrived right on time, accompanied by their lawyer. Tim wasn't surprised; the parents had seemed the sort to protect their own, as it should be. He just hoped that the kid was willing to talk to him, or them, or even the lawyer where Tim could hear.

Tim stood up and nodded to them as they filed in.

"Good morning." He offered his hand to the lawyer. "Constable Tim Geary."

The man shook his hand. "John Silvester."

"Have a seat." Tim looked at the boy, whose eyes were fixed on the floor. Tony Bell was seventeen, a senior at the high school, and he looked like he hadn't slept a lot the night before. "Mr. and Mrs. Bell. Thank you for coming in."

The parents nodded and sat down, Tony between them. Hell, none of them looked like they'd slept. Tim offered them all coffee and got three no-thank-yous, and sullen silence from Tony.

"Okay, let's begin, then." He sat down and reached for his voice recorder. "Everything is recorded, as I'm sure Mr. Silvester told you." When the parents had acknowledged that, Tim started the recorder and went through the entire spiel of the date, who was present, and the case file number. "Now. Mr. Silvester, before I start asking questions, does your client have any statements?"

Silvester looked at the kid, who kept staring sullenly at the table, and then up at the parents. The father nodded tightly; the mother looked like she was going to start crying.

"He does, but we need an agreement first, that should Tony make any sort of confession about this matter, you'll be lenient. No juvie. We feel that community service would be appropriate."

Tim's eyebrows shot up, the lawyer had to know better than that. Probably was posturing for the parents. "I don't hand down sentences, I just make recommendations. There is a lot more to this than punishment, you know that. At the very least, there will have to be some form of suggested psychiatric therapy to take to any judge."

Mrs. Bell did start crying then, her husband's arm going around her shoulder. Mr. Bell glared at the kid, a lot of anger in that look. "We already made him an appointment with a shrink before we left the hospital. Can we just do this?"

Silvester nodded. "Go ahead, Tony."

"It's not like I hurt people," Tony told the table.

"Tell me what you did do, then." Tim stomped down hard on his urge to lecture about how he had, in fact, hurt people.

Tony didn't say anything for a long moment. "That stupid dog next door. Barked all the time, day and night. I couldn't sleep. She wouldn't keep it in, she wouldn't stop it from making noise."

Tim opened the file with his notes and started hunting. "When was that, Tony?"

"About a month ago. Six weeks. I gave it some hamburger mixed up with the weed killer from our garage."

Mrs. Bell cried harder, little sobs that she was obviously trying to contain.

Silvester made notes and nodded at Tony. "Keep going, son."

Tim took notes and let the boy talk. Pets that had bitten, scratched, bothered him. Then pets of people who had insulted, yelled at, or teased him. And, finally, just pets. Because he could.

When Tony seemed to wind down, Tim went through his list, asking about animals that Tony hadn't mentioned. Bait had been left in places with no thought to specific creatures, near the end, and that just made it all the worse. Even Tony seemed to be grasping the enormity of what he'd done near the end. The lawyer looked grim, and Mrs. Bell has given up on wiping away tears.

Finally, Tim stood up. "Wait here," he said, as he gathered everything up. "There will be an officer outside the door, and I'll have sandwiches and coffee brought in while I'm preparing a statement for you to sign. Then you'll be placed under arrest and detained."

"Whatever."

Silvester's mouth tightened, his look becoming even grimmer. Mr. Bell couldn't seem to even look at his son anymore.

Tim looked at the lawyer. "I kind of suspect that your hopes for community service aren't going to go very far." He picked everything up and left, eager to be away from the angry, messed-up kid.

He arranged for food and coffee, then went right to his desk. He had a hell of a lot of notes to transcribe, but he really needed to talk to Ben, just to let him know. He just hoped Amy would put him right through.

"Terry Road Veterinary Clinic, how may I direct your call?"

"Good morning, I need to talk to Dr. Sauvigon, please. It's Constable Geary."

"Just a moment." The hold music came on and Tim blinked. Amy hadn't given him a second of guff. Maybe he was growing on her.

"Hi. Tim?" And she'd let Ben know who was on the phone, too. Wow.

"Hey, you. Did you yell at Amy or something?"

"What? No... was I supposed to?"

"No, no. It's just that she came startlingly close to being nice to me. Anyway, hi. I'm about to make an arrest and wanted to let you know."

"On the poisoning case? That's terrific!"

Tim nodded. "On the case. I can't give you any details at all, but I wanted to let you know for the peace of mind, you know?"

"Thanks, Tim. That's awesome. You'll have to come by after work this evening, so we can celebrate." He could hear the happiness in Ben's voice; he knew the increasing number of dead animals had been really bothering Ben.

"I'll do that." Tim smiled, and felt himself lighten a bit. "Do me a favor, though, and don't say anything to anyone about it for a couple of hours? I have to process paperwork before it's official."

"Mum's the word. And if anyone asks about the big grin on my face, I'll just tell them my boyfriend's coming over to fuck me through the mattress again tonight."

Tim laughed. "You do that. I'll see you later, okay?"

"Yeah, okay. And Tim? Thanks, man. That takes a load off."

"I know, Ben. Here, too." He thought about the boy in the interview room and sighed. "I need to get to work so this can be closed. Talk to you in a few hours."

"Yeah. I'll be the one waiting to tear your clothes off." With that, the line went dead.

Tim grinned. Someone really seemed to have enjoyed the night before. "Good to know," Tim said to himself as he turned to his computer and started writing up Tony's confession. "Very good to know."

Ben saw Anne Wilson and her two standard poodles out, and looked hopefully at what should have been an empty waiting room.

Except it wasn't. There was Missy Saunders and her pet bunny Fuzzles. Missy looked like she'd been crying, and Mrs. Saunders had a tight look on her face. Damn, he knew that look. He gave the bunny another once over and sighed. No twitching of ears or nose.

Damn it, he was supposed to be done with dead animals.

And he was supposed to be upstairs, waiting for Tim to get there so they could both ignore how hungry they were and get naked instead.

Stacey had called from the Bordon farm, though. She was going to be stuck out there all night with several cows who were calving and having a bad time of it, so he had to take her emergency duty.

And, it seemed, there were a lot of emergencies tonight.

He glanced at the clock. It was nearly eight. Damn it, he hoped that Tim hadn't come and gone already, that when he found Ben's place empty he'd try the clinic... He put a kind smile on his face and waved Missy, her mother, and the he-suspected-dead Fuzzles in.

An hour and two patients later, and the clinic waiting room was finally empty. He waved to the night desk clerk. "Call me if anyone comes in." And headed around back, wondering what had happened to Tim.

"Let me guess." The calm voice came from about halfway up the stairs, where Tim was sitting. "You didn't get to eat again."

"Eat? Is that that thing with the food and the filling of the empty belly? Because, no, I didn't do anything like that." He grinned, taking the stairs two at a time until he reached Tim.

"I brought you food." Tim cupped the back of his head with one hand, pulling him in for a kiss. "Big, huge submarine sandwiches."

He groaned as his cock and his stomach warred for dominance. "Is that a euphemism?" he asked as their lips parted.

"It wasn't." Tim laughed and climbed to his feet. "But I could make it one. Or I could blow you while you eat, I guess. Don't drip mustard on my head."

"I don't think I can eat and fuck at the same time. But submarines don't suffer from waiting." He took Tim's hand and led him up the rest of the stairs, making short work of the front door. Tippy barked happily at him and he opened the door again, letting her go out.

"I already ate." Tim pushed Ben against the doorframe and kissed him again. "Long day, Doc."

"Very long day. Are we celebrating?" He took another kiss before Tim could answer, grabbing Tim's waist and tugging him so their middles met.

"I am. Are you?" Tim rubbed against him like a big cat, his paws everywhere Ben could want them to be. "Arrest made. The rest is out of my hands."

"That's fantastic!" He laughed and pushed back against Tim. "I might have gone out at lunch and bought champagne."

Tim stared at him. "Are you serious? Wow. Pop that cork!"

"Now, *that* has to be a euphemism." Or maybe Ben was just really horny.

"Yeah, it was." Tim grinned and started working on Ben's buttons.

"Yes!" He laughed, touching Tim wherever he could.

"Stop that." Tim batted his hands away and rubbed a bit harder. "I can't get in your pants when you're distracting me like that." Which was a total *lie*, since Tim's hand was right then curling around Ben's cock.

He groaned, pushing into Tim's touch.

Tippy whined at the door and Ben laughed again. "Fuck. I need to let her in." Which he totally couldn't do shoved up against the door like this.

"Okay, but she can't watch." Tim stroked him again and let him go, backing off just enough for Ben to get to the door.

He opened it and closed it again as soon as she came in. It slammed up against his back again and he tugged Tim to him. "Make me come."

Tim dropped to his knees and took him in, sucking

hard and looking up. His eyes were wide open, his lips swollen from just their few kisses, and his hands were tugging Ben's trousers down over his hips.

Ben whimpered, pushing in deeper, loving the way Tim just opened up to him.

Licking and suckling, Tim kept staring up him, his head bobbing slowly. When Tim's hands slid up to Ben's ass and urged him to move, it was clear that Ben was being invited to take whatever he needed.

He wrapped his hands around Tim's head, holding it as he started to thrust. *Oh, damn.* That was too good. Crying out, he started to move faster.

Tim hummed and closed his eyes, opening wider. When Ben's cock hit what had to be the back of Tim's throat, Tim moaned and his fingers dug in deep.

"Tim! Tim! Shit." He lost it, come shooting out of him.

Fingers digging in so hard they must have left bruises, Tim took it and swallowed, again and again, before he pulled away, panting. "Oh, God. Ben. Yes."

"Uh-huh." He slid down the door, grinning at Tim when he landed. "Thanks."

"That cork really popped." Tim made a show of trying to catch his breath. "God. Poor Tippy looks traumatized."

"She is *not* looking." And neither was he. He was not going to look and see those long, floppy ears and those sad eyes.

"If you say so." Tim was laughing at him. Or maybe with him. He looked happy, anyway. "Are you hungry now?"

"I was hungry before, now I'm starving." He brought their mouths together, tasting himself on Tim's lips. "What about you?"

"I ate, but I'll take a beer if you have one. Or that

champagne."

"I meant the other hungry." He reached for Tim's crotch, groping around.

"Oh, *that*!" Tim helped, ripping his button-fly jeans open. "Go."

Ben half snorted, half laughed, fingers wrapping around Tim's heat. "Is she watching?" he asked, lips still twitching.

"Who?" Tim suddenly sounded breathless again, and his hips were twitching.

"Tippy."

"Tippy?" Tim's head fell back with a thunk. "Ben. Don't tease."

"Hey, you started it. Telling me she looked traumatized." He kept stroking Tim's prick. He wasn't teasing.

"Fuck." Tim gasped, and his hips did more than twitch as he started thrusting into Ben's hand. "Oh, God. Oh, God, yes. Ben." His right thigh was starting to shake, and his cock was leaking over Ben's fingers.

"You're pretty hot for it." Ben didn't figure it would take Tim long to blow.

"Hot for you." Tim thrust again, and one of his hands landed on the floor with a smack. Using that arm for leverage, Tim grunted and arched, his cock pulsing as he started to shoot.

"Pretty. So pretty." Ben squeezed his hand tight.

"Ben!" Tim yelled loudly with the rest of his orgasm, his whole body shaking with it and the tendons in his neck standing out. "Ben." As soon as his prick stopped throbbing, Tim was reaching for him.

Ben pushed into Tim's lap, the two of them collapsing on the floor in a heap. He had an elbow in his side, but he couldn't be bothered to move.

"Thanks," Tim whispered, kissing him softly. "I

Once Upon a Veterinarian

missed you today."

"Yeah, I missed you, too. I kept having to stop myself from calling and finding out what was up." He nuzzled against Tim. "Did you say you had food? Phallic-shaped food at that?"

"Only the best for my baby." Tim laughed softly and nodded. "Phallic-shaped food, right here. I hope we didn't squish it on the way to the floor." He was patting around beside him, and the crinkle of paper declared his success. "Oh, not bad. Okay, time for supper."

He started opening a sandwich and Tippy barked, coming over to see what kind of food there was.

"Not for you," Tim said. He patted around again. "This is for you." He tossed a rawhide strip onto the floor, a foot or so away from Tippy. "Good girl."

"Hey! You brought my dog a bone." He gave Tim a hard kiss. "That's pretty special."

He wasn't sure, but he thought maybe Tim was blushing. "Yeah, well. She's a good dog. And I like her owner a lot."

"Yeah, you must." He gave Tim a kiss, grinning. "I like you a lot, too."

Tim nuzzled his jaw. "Eat. See, Tippy knows what to do with a treat. I'm going to go wash up."

"Are you trying to say I'm not as smart as my dog?"

"I'm trying to say that you're going to starve to death, and then I'll have a dead boyfriend and you won't be any good to me at all." Tim beamed at him and kissed his nose.

He blinked and then laughed, taking a bite of his sandwich. "There. See? No dead boyfriend."

"Awesome. Don't choke, either. I've got more stuff to feed you when you're done." Tim winked and rolled away, then struggled to stand up while his pants were mostly down.

"More stuff to feed me?" Ben's eyebrows went up, then his eyes narrowed. "Like what? Oh, this is good. I like the tangy sauce on it."

"Like what?" Tim rinsed his hands at the sink and examined his clothes, probably for messes that were not made of tangy sauce. "Well, let's just say that the next time I get off, I hope I won't have to check my clothes for come stains."

"You're a pushy lover, you know that?" He grinned around his next bite.

"Yeah." Tim got himself all put away and neat, then sat back down with him. "But you like that. I can tell." His foot rubbed playfully along Ben's.

"Maybe. Just a little." He grinned. "It'll be interesting to see how you taste with the champagne."

"How would that work, exactly?" Tim tilted his head and looked intrigued. "Body shots?"

"I was more thinking in my mouth at the same time. All those bubbles..."

"Ohhh." Tim's eyes went wide. "Oh, man. Hurry up and eat. Yeah, that'd be *awesome*."

"You're a perv, too. Pushy and a perv." Which made Ben pretty lucky.

"You just promised me bubbles on my *cock*. Do you think I'm gonna turn that down?" Tim laughed and looked at Tippy. "He's crazy. Come live with me."

"No stealing my girl." He gave Tim a wink. God, look at them -- on the floor, he still wasn't put away right, and talking about blowjobs with champagne.

Life was good.

Chapter Nineteen

Tim's week got better with each day. Granted, it wasn't even Thursday, but he'd stopped a kid from killing pets, he'd gotten that curse well and truly broken, and he'd finally had a day when work ended when it was supposed to.

"So, supper out or in?" He was happy to stay on the couch and kiss for a bit, but eventually they'd need to eat.

"Let's order something greasy and unhealthy." Ben wandered out of the kitchen with a couple of bottles of water, and grabbed the remote before joining him on the non-Tippy end of the couch.

"I do love the way you think. Burgers or pizza?" Tim took the first of what he hoped would be many kisses along with the bottle of water.

That first kiss turned into a second, Ben not answering his question in favor of shoving his tongue down Tim's throat. Tim approved. A lot. He worked one hand up the inside of Ben's shirt and tweaked a nipple, then headed back down to slide his fingers under the waistband of Ben's pants.

Ben made a happy, horny little noise, fingers clutching at his T-shirt. "I can't think when you do that."

"Who needs to think?" Tim played a little more, then felt up Ben's ass, his fingers pushing at the seam of Ben's pants. "Want."

"Uh-huh. Let's get the edge off first, though. And have supper. And watch a movie or something." There was an evil glint in Ben's eyes.

"I'm all edges. Which one are we going to start with? Hand edge? Mouth? Wanna rub off on me?" Oh, man, he was going to drive himself insane.

"I like this edge." Ben's hand slid down Tim's chest and rubbed at the bulge in his jeans, fingers playing lightly.

"It's a favorite of mine," Tim agreed happily. "Oh, man. You're teasing again."

"You know, any time I touch you and we're not naked, you say I'm only teasing."

"We should totally be naked all the time. Just to save the stress, you know?"

"I keep telling you, I don't want Tippy seeing me naked."

Tim tried to get more kissing and more naked, but Ben was being stubborn on both counts. "We can blindfold her," he suggested.

Ben started laughing. "Oh, man, what did I ever do for fun before you showed up in my life?"

"I have no idea." Tim felt heat blossom in his belly. "Probably the same boring stuff I did without you."

"Oh, I don't work out." Ben grinned smugly.

"But you like that I do." Tim was just as smug as he flexed.

"I do." Ben nodded, eyes on Tim's belly as he tugged his T-shirt up. "I really do."

"I like that you like it." Really, really a lot. It was nice to be admired, to feel attractive. It was nice that

Ben wanted him. That it was Ben made it important and special.

Bending, Ben licked his abs. "Hold that thought." Then Ben was up off the couch and headed for the door.

"What? Wait! Huh?" Tim watched him go and then looked at Tippy. "Crazy."

Ben went to the door and started calling for Tippy. "Hey, girl. Come on. Time to go out for a while."

Tippy woofed and got up slowly, ambling toward the door.

"Oh, right. No naked, no blindfold. Can we be naked now?" Tim was already undoing his fly.

"You can be. I wanna suck you." Ben closed the door behind Tippy and came back to the couch, eyes on his middle.

"I have no issues with that." None. Not one. In fact, he had his hand in his pants, tugging his cock free. "Ready!"

Ben slapped at his hand. "I wanted to do that!"

Tim stuffed it back in. "Go for it. But hurry, it's getting confused."

Laughing his head off, Ben went to his knees in front of Tim. "Crazy perv."

"Tease. And always with the name-calling!" Tim couldn't stop smiling. "Got a present for you there in my pants."

"I can see that. And you're pretty free with the name-calling yourself." Ben licked a circle around Tim's navel, and then followed the path of his abs.

"Tease. Lover. Baby. Oh, man. Do that again."

"This?" Ben nibbled this time, still following the lines of his abs, going right down to his waistband.

"Yes, that!" Tim had no idea what to do with his hands, so he held onto the couch back with one and brushed Ben's hair with the other. "Licking is good, too.

And kissing. Kissing is nice."

Ben laughed, his breath warm against Tim's skin. "Pushy, pushy."

Before Tim could reply or get indignant or anything, Ben undid his top button again, slowly pulling down his zipper.

"That's it," Tim whispered. "God, I love your mouth. Come on, give it to me."

He could feel Ben smile against his skin, and then his jeans were pulled open, Ben licking the hollow next to his hip.

Tim gasped and tried to hold himself very still as his cock lifted and flexed. "You're going to drive me crazy."

"Won't have far to go, then." Ben gave him a wink and a quick kiss to the tip of his cock before giving the dip by his other hip the same nibble and lick. Only slower this time.

"Ben." Tim dragged the name out until it filled his entire breath. "Please. Suck me."

"I am sucking you." Ben's mouth opened over his hipbones, suction starting, pulling at his skin.

Tim growled. Then he yelled, "Suck my *cock*!" He hoped he'd made his point through his laughter.

Ben seemed to be honestly trying now, though he was having a hard time closing his mouth around the snorts and giggles.

"You know, I can coach you through it." Tim reached down and held his prick with one hand. "See? Now it won't move. You suck this part here." He pointed.

Ben laughed harder and slapped at his hand. "I do know what I'm doing, here." Ben's fingers slid over his skin, teasing the slit and spreading the single drop of pre-come that had leaked out.

Slowly, too damn slowly, if you asked Tim, Ben bent to his prick.

"Did he leave you out here all by yourself? You poor thing?" That could only be Stacey's voice, and given the low woof that followed, she had to be talking to Tippy.

Ben jerked, leaping to his feet just as a knock came, followed by Stacey opening the door. "Ben, you big meanie, you left your dog out."

Tim shoved his cock in his pants and stood, back to the door. "She was out for a reason," he called, fighting with his zipper.

"Oh, Tim, hi there. I didn't realize you were visiting."

He could hear Ben head to the door, slowing Stacey's progress coming in. "Hi, Stacey, Tippy was out getting some air. What's up?"

"I brought food and a bottle of wine. I thought we could celebrate the brilliant capture of the poisoner. So I'm glad you're here, Tim. You deserve most of the credit, I believe."

"Stacey." Tim nodded and smiled at her. "We were.... uh, having our own little celebration, actually."

"Oh, I'd have thought you'd have done that already." She laughed and came on in, the door closing behind her. "You haven't eaten yet, have you?"

"No, we haven't, and that smells really good." Ben's stomach growled loudly, giving credence to his words.

It did, actually. Maybe even better than pizza. Still, Tim raised an eyebrow as she headed to the table. "Um, come on in, I guess." Did she ever actually wait for an invitation?

At least she didn't sit on the couch, pulling up a chair instead. "Get some plates and forks, Ben. It's from that new Greek place. Oh, and some glasses for the wine."

Ben ran his hand through his hair, the dark blush starting to fade out of his cheeks. "Okay."

"I'll get the glasses." Tim headed into the kitchen,

grateful for the time alone to readjust what was going on in his pants. Or what *had* been going on. Nothing killed a boner like unexpected company.

Ben joined him a moment later, pulling down plates and grabbing forks and knives. "At least we don't have to worry about starving now."

Tim looked at him. "We weren't going to starve," he pointed out. He also helped himself to the wine. "Thanks, Stacey."

She poured out two more glasses, Ben taking the second. "Help yourselves, boys. I got a little bit of everything."

"Calamari?" Ben asked, sounding hopeful.

Tim sat back in his chair and watched Ben dive into the calamari. It was pretty cute, really. Almost cute enough to get him past his irritation. After all, she wasn't going to stay all night, was she? He could eat her food and drink her wine.

Then he could wave goodbye and drag Ben off to bed, where Tippy wouldn't be watching them get back to business.

He could do that just fine.

Ben was half asleep by the time Stacey wound down and headed off, patting his cheek gently. "Go to bed, Ben." Her eyes twinkled. "And your boyfriend, too."

His cheeks heated a little and he rolled his eyes. "Good night, Stacey."

She laughed and kissed his cheek before waving at Tim. "Good night, Ben. Good night, Officer."

"Night, Stacey." Tim stayed where he was, sprawled on the couch, though he did wave.

"You need to go out again, Tippy?" Her ears didn't

even twitch. "Okay, that's a no." He locked up behind Stacey and stretched. "Oh. I kind of assumed you could stay..."

"I'm not leaving." Tim grinned up at him. "I was hoping we could pick up where we left off. You know. Before she invited herself in to join the party."

"I *was* blowing you, wasn't I?" He reached out, offering his hand. "Come to bed. That way if I fall asleep halfway through it, at least we're both lying down."

Tim laughed. "No falling asleep in the middle! That would really be horrible. I'll see if I can keep you interested, okay?" He took Ben's hand and pulled himself up. "Hey, you."

"Hey. And I'm betting you can. Keep me interested, that is." He kept hold of Tim's hand, leading him to the bedroom.

"As long as no one shows up at the door, anyway." Tim laughed as he went with Ben, giving his hand a squeeze. "She really has no idea, does she?"

"Huh? Stacey? She won't be coming back tonight."

Tim snorted as he let go of Ben's hand to start undressing. "Not tonight, no. But she'll have bad timing again. It's her thing, you know?"

"I didn't used to have guests in the evening." Hell, it was still unusual enough to have Tim over -- they didn't seem to be able to manage two nights in a row very often.

"But now you do." Tim said it easily enough, and he was shirtless, his fingers working on his pants. "Um, are we going to bed, Mr. Still Dressed?"

"Yes, we're going to bed, Mr. Could Be Helping Me."

Tim laughed and shoved his pants down, then pounced. "I got myself undressed. I can get you undressed, too, but that tends to lead to both of us rubbing and licking and stuff, and I really, really missed getting that blowjob. Kiss me?"

Laughing, Ben did just that, reaching for Tim, finding a hip and that hot, eager cock.

Tim's hands fumbled a bit, and the kiss was sloppy, since they were both laughing and grinning, but, bit by bit, clothes came undone, and there were Tim's hands on him, and Tim's sounds filling the room.

"If you want that blowjob, we'd better hit the bed." Because in about two seconds, he was going to forget about everything but getting off.

Tim didn't even let him go, just got them turned around and tugged him right down onto the end of the bed. "Please? Ben, please. No teasing at all, just -- " He was flatteringly out of words as he scrambled up the bed.

Ben crawled up between Tim's legs, intent on that hard cock. He could do no teasing.

"Yes, yes, yes." Tim's fingers slid over his hair, across his cheeks, and finally grabbed the blanket. "Now. Please." His cock was standing away from his body, wet at the tip.

"Like, right now?" He wasn't teasing, though, not really, his mouth dropping down over Tim's prick, his cheeks already hollowed out as he started sucking.

"Fuck, yes." Tim's whole body went tight for a moment, then relaxed. "God, I love your mouth," he murmured. His hips were already pushing, his cock gliding in and out of Ben's mouth.

Ben let Tim do what he wanted -- he'd take his time to taste and explore and tease next time.

Panting, Tim kept going, one leg sliding on the bed until he found a way to get some leverage. "God. Ben." His voice was rough, and Ben had to wonder just how long Tim had been working himself up for this.

His head bobbed, his hand finding Tim's balls and rolling them.

Tim made an inarticulate noise and his hands landed on Ben's head, petting and finally holding on. Not too hard, but he was definitely holding Ben where he wanted him while he got closer and closer to coming.

Ben nodded a little, trying to let Tim know to take what he wanted.

"Ben!" Tim shoved in hard and fast, fucking his mouth rapidly for a half dozen strokes before he went still, his cock flexing as he started to come.

Ben swallowed, taking the bitter, salty liquid in, and pulling on Tim's cock for more.

"Love you," Tim whispered weakly, his whole body going lax.

Ben froze and looked up, meeting Tim's eyes. "What?"

Tim blinked blearily at him. "What what? Is that bad?"

"No. Not bad. Say it again."

Tim gave him a slow smile. "I love you."

He could feel a matching smile starting inside him at Tim's words. "That's what I thought you said."

"I can say it again, if you want." Tim tugged at his arm, urging him up closer.

"Okay." He slid up and pushed against Tim's hip, rubbing and leaking on the warm skin.

"I love you." Tim's hand wrapped around his hip, holding him close.

"Good. Because I think I love you, too."

"That's kind of important," Tim whispered, still smiling at him.

"Uh-huh." His own smile was getting bigger every moment, his hips moving and pushing, getting friction for his erection.

"Want a hand with that? I love you."

"Uh-huh. Please." He grabbed Tim's hand and dragged it to his prick.

Tim took him in hand and started stroking, not looking away from his eyes. "Love the way you feel, and the way you taste, and the way you think. Love the way you gasp when I do this."

Ben gasped, just like Tim said he loved, not able to stop himself.

"That's it." Tim kept on petting, and kept on stroking, and kept on talking. "I love the sound of your voice, the smell of your skin. I love your dog, even. I love your compassion and your strength. And I love the way you look at me when you come."

"Tim!" He cried out, hips bucking, pushing his cock through Tim's hand as he came.

"That." Tim kissed him hard, tasting and loving him all the way through it.

He sank against Tim when he was done. "Hey." He smiled at Tim, feeling great. "Love you."

Tim kissed him again, a lot softer. "Love you. Tell me again in the morning."

"It's a deal."

He was still smiling, warm all the way through, as he fell asleep.

Chapter Twenty

Tim checked his look in the mirror more times than he cared to admit. He changed his tie twice, but only back and forth. It wasn't like he owned a selection of ties, just the two. But the darker one looked better, classy and sharp, so he went with it. The tie might have changed, but the smile stayed the same.

He'd had perma-grin for three days.

It hadn't gone unnoticed at work, either, and while the guys were all rolling their eyes about him finally getting laid, it was Heather who pinned him to a wall and demanded to know when he'd fallen in love.

Tim told her it was about four minutes after he met Ben, he just hadn't known it at the time.

Then he'd asked her to trade shifts with him, so he could take Ben on a real date. She said he was a sneaky bastard, but she traded, and now here he was. In a suit, and going to pick up Ben for dinner at a fancy restaurant with actual linens on the table.

He drove to the clinic and parked, hoping Ben managed to end the day on time and thus would be all set to go; Tim wasn't exactly clear on how reservations worked, but he was pretty sure they wouldn't hold the table forever.

He could hear laughter as he climbed the stairs. Definitely female-sounding laughter.

Great. Oh, well, she'd just have to deal. They had reservations. Still grinning, Tim knocked at the door and opened it up, making sure not to let Tippy out. "Hey, you two."

"Hey, Tim. Wow, nice threads." Stacey looked him up and down. "Very fancy."

Ben, dressed in jeans and a T-shirt, got up and came toward him, smiling and happy and giving him a hug and a kiss. "Hey. You do look really good."

"Um, thanks." Tim kissed him back and gave him a half smile. "How long until you'll be ready, babe? We're going to be late."

"Oh, well, here's the thing."

Before Ben could finish, Stacey broke in. "It's been a long couple of days at the clinic and I figured Ben needed to unwind. Hell, we both do, so I brought dinner, wine and some movies."

Ben gave him helpless shrug. "You don't mind, do you?"

"Yes." Tim shook his head. "I do mind, Ben. We have plans."

Ben took a step back, blinking. "Oh. I didn't think you'd mind. I mean, we can go to dinner another night, right?"

"Come on, Timmy, don't be a spoilsport -- me dropping by with dinner and movies is a bit of a tradition around here."

Tim stared at them both. "Okay, can I talk to you alone for a minute, Ben?" Tradition? Fuck that. He was dating Ben, not the Ben and Stacey Team Event.

"Sure..." Ben looked from him to Stacey and back

again, a small frown on his face.

Stacey snorted and waved. "Go on and make kissy face in the other room, but if I eat all the shrimp kung pao, don't blame me."

Tim headed into the bedroom, all but dragging Ben with him. "Why is she here?" he asked as soon as the door closed. "You knew we were going out for something special. She always does this, and you let her."

"What? She does not always do it. Only when work's been rough. And of course I let her, we're friends and we help each other out. I honestly thought you wouldn't mind -- we can do dinner another night."

Tim shook his head. "You blew me off to unwind with her once when you needed to, I get that. But she walks in, she takes over, you actually let her intrude in the middle of a fucking blowjob, Ben! I went to a lot of effort for tonight, and just because she's decided to watch a movie with you, you're going to blow me off again? No. No way. Who are you dating?" Tim could hear his voice rising, but he was helpless to stop it.

"You, Tim. You know that. I mean I told you I lo--." Ben's mouth snapped shut. "Am I supposed to give up my other friends because I'm dating you, is that it?"

"No!" Tim ran his hand through his hair. "But you don't let her take over our dates. You don't choose her over me. That's all. Look at me. I'm wearing a fucking tie for you, and you couldn't tell her that tomorrow was better for movies? You had other plans? Or do the plans with me come second to her?"

"Of course not! I didn't realize this date was such a big deal. I mean, we spend all our free time together, right?" Ben looked miserable.

"Only when she lets us!" Tim put a hand on Ben's shoulder. "Look. She needs to back off. You need to decide what you want. And I need to go. Call me tomorrow."

"You're *going*? Why can't the three of us just watch movies? Are you saying you won't spend time with me if Stacey's around?" Ben lowered his voice. "You dislike her that much?"

Tim shook his head again. "You're not hearing what I'm saying. I don't dislike her at all. I *like* her. But she's not a part of you and me, and you're both treating me with a bit of disrespect by continually having her take over our time together. We can spend a lot of time with her, I'd like that. But I'm not canceling plans you and I have so she can force us to do what *she* wants."

"So you want me to go out there and tell her to come back some other night?"

"Yes." Finally. "That's what I want. And then I want you in a suit so we can go to dinner."

"She's not going to be very happy about this," muttered Ben, turning to go.

"Would you rather have her nose out of joint or me being hurt and not here?" Tim asked bluntly. "This is a big deal, Ben. Think about it, please. Right now. You had your mouth on my cock and you let her in. She flat-out told me, not five minutes ago, to come in here and make kissy faces. She doesn't see what she's doing as intruding. You don't, either. But you know what? She is. Look, never mind. I'm too pissed to make a decent night of it at this point. I'm going home. Call me later, after your movies."

"*Anybody* could have knocked on the door and that blowjob would have been over, and you know it! And, okay, maybe I should have told her we had a date, but that's true any night we're both off, and I didn't realize tonight was so important to you. Tim..."

Tim headed for the door. "No, Ben. I don't know that. *I* would have yelled at whoever the hell it was to come back later. *I* would have told my buddy that I had a hot date. *I* wouldn't presume that a change of plans to include my friend all the time was okay. *I* am going home."

"You're blowing this all out of proportion, so maybe you should."

"Right." Tim opened the door and headed down the hall. "Call me when you sort out your fucking priorities."

"Tim..."

Ben's words were drowned out by Stacey. "Uh-oh, that doesn't sound good."

"You." Tim turned and glared at her. "Look around. See what's going on. And then take into account that sometimes traditions need to change." Without waiting for her reply, he left, slamming the door behind him.

Screw going home. He was heading to the nearest bar, and there was no way in hell he was answering his phone before morning.

Chapter Twenty-One

Ben listened to the sound of the door slamming, trying to figure out what the hell had just happened. He went slowly back into the living room, Tippy huffing and howling a little, picking up on the negative vibes. Of which there were plenty.

"What the hell is his problem?" Stacey had a fork full of kung pao half way to her mouth. "He really needs to chill out."

"I guess... I don't know." Tim's words buzzed around in his head, and he sat miserably next to Tippy, fondling her ears.

She snorted. "Honestly, is he always so cranky? I don't see what you see in him, if so. He's always so uptight."

"Tim's not uptight. Well, not usually. You've just only seen him when..." When she'd interrupted them in the middle of something or a date.

"When he's in a bad mood?" She shoved a Chinese take-out container into his hand. "Come on, eat with me."

He grabbed the box automatically, but he didn't feel very much like eating. At all. "No, it's not that. He said I keep putting you ahead of him."

Was that true; was he doing that?

"What? That's crazy." She shook her head and kept on eating. "Honestly. How is that possibly true? Does he want you to spend every minute of your time alone with him? That's just not realistic."

"That's what *I* said."

"Right." She nodded as if the whole matter was settled. "So then he stormed out. Nice. Well, his loss."

"What's that supposed to mean?" It felt a hell of a lot more like *his* loss than Tim's. Or maybe both their losses.

"What's what supposed to mean?" She gave him an odd look. "He lost his temper about not getting you all to himself, and now he's missing out on movies and take-out."

"Well, yeah, but we were supposed to be going out for a dinner date, and we're both missing out on that."

Maybe he was starting to see why Tim had been upset. He still thought Tim had overreacted, but he could have told Stacey he was busy. Come to think of it, he had said that when she'd first arrived, and she'd said Tim wouldn't mind.

She gave him a long look and chewed slowly. "You said your plans weren't that important. That it was *just* dinner."

"I guess I didn't realize how important they were to Tim. We don't actually go out-out all that often, because you never know when something's going to come up." Had he chosen Stacey over Tim? He was just so used to going with the flow, to following along with whatever Stacey set up.

Stacey stuck her fork in her container and frowned. "What else did he say, Ben? I mean, exactly. Because he hardly ever seems thrilled with me, but you seem to think he's awesome. What am I missing?"

"Well, he pointed out that." He cleared his throat, starting to blush and finished the rest really quickly. "You interrupted a blowjob the other day, and I didn't say anything to try to get you to go home instead of stay."

Her jaw dropped open. "I what? When? Oh my God!" She hit him on the arm with a solid thunk. "Ben! Good lord, no wonder he's cranky!"

"Ow! Well, what was I supposed to do? *Tell* you we were in the middle of things? The mood was already broken."

"*Yes*!" She waved her hand around and almost spilled the kung pao. "A very strong 'Hey, Stace, we're getting busy here, come back in an hour' would work wonders! Jesus, Ben!" He'd never seen her blush before. He hadn't known she *could* blush.

He groaned, holding his head in his hands. "I've screwed up, haven't I?"

"Slightly." She sighed and forked more kung pao into her mouth. "But I think I helped."

He bit his lip, trying to look at things from Tim's point of view. The truth was that this week wasn't the only time Stacey had come around when they were together. Now that he thought about it, she was part of the reason the 'curse' had lasted so long.

"I should call him and apologize, eh?" He wondered if Tim liked his blowjobs enough that he could use them to barter his way back into the man's good graces.

"Uh-huh. Although he didn't look like he was in the mood to answer." She sighed again and looked at him. "I'm sorry, Ben. I'm not used to you having a life other than work and hanging out with me."

"I should be able to still hang out with you -- I've always disliked it when people dropped their friends as soon as they had a boyfriend or girlfriend." But that didn't mean there couldn't be boundaries set, and it looked like he'd just ignored a pretty important one. "Maybe I should ask you to call before coming over, though."

She nodded. "And when I get here I should knock, not just come in." She looked into her kung pao and frowned. "Maybe if he has some warning, he won't mind me so much. Because I'm not going anywhere."

"He does like you, Stacey, he said so. It's me he's mad at." Oh, God, what was he going to do to?

"Where did he go? Did he say? Maybe you can find him?"

"I have no idea where he went -- home, I think. I'll call him." He grabbed the phone and dialed Tim's number, groaning when it went over to voicemail. "Um, Tim? It's me, Ben. Are you there? If you're there, pick up, okay? You told me to call you when... when I got my priorities straight. And I have. I've figured it out, okay? I'm sorry. Please pick up?"

He waited a moment longer and then sighed and hung up. "He's not home. Or he doesn't want to talk to me."

"Okay." Stacey sat up and looked like she was ready for business. "So, tonight, we plan. Something special, for him. Suit, dinner, the works. Romance, Benji. Let's go."

"Let me try his cell phone first." He dialed that and it went to voicemail immediately, meaning Tim had turned it off. "I guess he *really* doesn't want to talk to me." He sighed and nodded. "It had better be *very* romantic, Stacey. I really like him."

"I kind of suck at romance. But there's always the internet and the phone book. First, dinner. Nicest place you can think of, or something catered here?" She went to his kitchen and rummaged around, finally producing a pad of paper and a pen. "And roses."

She might have been a part of the problem, but Ben

was really glad Stacey was here to help him with the solution. No one got things done better than Stacey on a mission.

He just hoped Tim would accept his apology.

Chapter Twenty-Two

Tim spent a horrible night out, sulking in a bar full of cops who seemed to know better than to even try to talk to him. One of them -- and God, he had no idea who -- drove him home and poured him into bed.

He'd sooner cut off his tongue than miss work the next morning, though. Not after Heather had traded shifts for him. He dressed, he ate, and he spent the whole day being cranky and nursing a headache.

He listened to Ben's voice mail a million times, but he didn't call him back. Not when he was on shift and couldn't really deal with anything. He had to wonder, though, what had happened after he'd left.

When his shift was done, Tim didn't waste any time going home. He needed to change and nap in the worst way, and then maybe -- maybe -- he'd call Ben back.

He pulled up into his driveway to find Ben sitting on his steps, wearing a suit and holding what looked suspiciously like a bouquet of flowers.

Tim sat in his car and stared for a moment, then got out. "Um. Hi."

"Hi, there." Ben came down off the stairs to meet him, waving the purple paper-wrapped packet at him. "These are for you. Oh, and so are these." A box of Godiva chocolates was shoved at him.

"Um." Wow, beer in large quantities seemed to make him stupid. "Thank you. You look nice. I was going to call you back." He held the chocolates and wondered what he was supposed to do next.

"Those are roses. Two dozen long-stemmed roses with the thorns removed. Red ones. Expensive. Really expensive. The chocolate-covered cherries were, too. Because I'm sorry. I really am."

Tim stared and blinked and stared some more. "Uh, thank you. Again. You... I guess you thought about stuff, huh?" The roses smelled really good. "No one's ever given me flowers before."

"No? They should have. You deserve flowers. And, yeah, I thought about stuff, and I talked with Stacey and she says she's sorry, too. She's going to call from now on. Before coming over." Ben looked around. "Do you think we could do the rest of this inside?"

Tim nodded, still feeling faintly stunned. He had expected an apology, given the voicemail, and he'd known it was going to blow over. But he hadn't expected this. "Sure. Inside." He led the way, then had to fumble around for his keys. "Stacey's going to call first? That'd be awesome. Is she really pissed at me?"

"No. She was kind of ticked off at me, though. She even walloped me."

Tim opened the door and let Ben walk in past him. "She what?" Okay, that was unexpected. He led Ben all the way up all four flights of stairs, still trying to get his head wrapped around the fact that he was holding roses and chocolates. "Let me put these in water."

"Yeah. Apparently I was supposed to blurt out that

she was interrupting a blowjob. I'm still not so sure about that one, but I definitely could have told her we wanted to be alone, and I should have been more insistent that last night was a special date and we'd have to reschedule movies."

Ben grabbed his arms and looked into his eyes. "I really am sorry, Tim. You *are* my priority. I won't give up my friends, but they should understand that you come first and sometimes we need time for just us."

Well. That was... pretty much exactly what Tim wanted to hear. And Ben was wearing a suit and he'd brought roses and chocolate and his best friend apparently got it, too. "I love you," Tim said softly. "Thank you. I'm sorry I got mad."

"No, you don't have to apologize for that. I was being stupid and I wasn't thinking."

"But you are now." Tim looked him up and down and smiled. "I think my headache is going away. Fast."

"Yeah?" Ben gave him a warm smile. "I thought if you wanted we could go out somewhere fancy tonight. To make up for yesterday."

Tim nodded and then looked at himself, reluctant to look away from Ben in a *suit*. "I need to shower in the worst way. We don't have reservations anywhere." He hoped his suit wasn't a mess; he didn't exactly remember hanging it up.

"I suppose we could stay in instead." Ben leaned a little toward him, and then stopped.

"The roses need water." What the hell? Tim could practically feel his brain melting. "I really like your suit." A lot. A lot, a lot.

"Thanks." Ben took a deep breath. "Can we kiss and make up now? Please?"

Tim darted forward. He dropped the chocolates, and the roses were crushed between them as he plunged his tongue into Ben's mouth. He'd been aching all day, worried and upset, and now it was done and over. Now he could just go back to loving his man and being happy.

Ben's mouth opened wide, arms wrapping around him and pulling him in even closer. It was a good thing the roses didn't have thorns.

"I'm sorry I yelled," Tim said into the kiss. The words were garbled, but maybe Ben would figure it out on his own. Tim kept kissing him, wishing he could at least pull some sense together and get his heavy belt and gun off. But Ben tasted so good, and the roses smelled so sweet. Oh, God, the roses. He wondered if they'd stain Ben's suit.

"Bedroom?" Ben asked, eyes hot, wanting.

"Anywhere." Tim nodded and moved back enough to undo his belt, barely saving the roses from hitting the floor or landing on the chocolates. "I'll find something to put these in later." Much later.

"They'll keep." Ben grabbed his collar and started backing him down the hall. "I thought I'd lost you."

"No way." Tim shook his head and moved with Ben. "Even cranky, I'm still yours. Promise. I don't throw away good things."

"Thank God." Ben dragged him right into his own bedroom, kissing and nibbling at his lips.

Tim was happy enough to be manhandled; his cock even seemed to be really liking it. Ben backed him to the bed and Tim couldn't get his pants undone fast enough. Then he got distracted by Ben's tie, and had to hold onto it for a minute while he kissed Ben hard. "Too many clothes."

"Yeah. Yeah, I was trying to look as hot as you did last night."

"You're hotter." Ben's suit was a lot nicer, and Ben was just so much more *Ben*. Tim slid his hands inside

Ben's jacket and across his chest. "God." His cock was going to actually rip right out of his pants, he just knew it.

"No way, you are. In or out of a suit." Ben tugged at his clothes, fingers fumbling with buttons.

"We are not going to fight about this." Tim gasped and shoved at Ben's jacket. "For God's sake!" Maybe it would work better if they just undressed themselves.

Ben obviously had the same idea, because he pushed Tim's hands away and shrugged out of his jacket, tugging at his tie. "Keep that close."

Tim's sturdy uniform fabric could withstand a bit of abuse, so he skipped over a few buttons and tugged his shirt off over his head, then kicked off his shoes.

Laughing at him, Ben pulled the tie off and then his shirt and pants followed, leaving Ben standing there in his boxers and socks.

"That'll do. Well, maybe not the socks." Tim shed his pants like they were a snakeskin, his briefs going with them, and the socks following within seconds. "I'll keep your feet warm."

"I hope you'll keep what's under the shorts warm, too!"

Tim grinned and stretched out on the bed. "You should probably put it somewhere."

"Yeah? Like..." Looking happy, Ben dragged the boxers down and off, his prick standing up at attention.

With one hand, Tim reached under his pillow for the lube. Then he rolled over.

"Oh. Oh, yes." He felt the bed dip as Ben climbed up, taking the lube from him, hands sliding on his ass.

Tim arched, his shoulders low and his ass high. "Please, Ben." He wanted. God, he wanted. He *needed*.

Ben's fingers were shaking a little as they slid along his crack. "Want you."

Tim nodded and held onto the comforter. "Want you, too. Always. Need you, Ben."

Ben's finger pushed into him, spreading him. Another was quickly added. "Don't want to wait."

"Don't." Tim was reduced to whispers. His eyes closed and he rocked back, wanting more. The slight stretch wasn't enough; he needed Ben to fill him up. "Don't wait. Please."

Ben's fingers slid away. He had to wait as long as it took for Ben to put on the condom, and then the heat of Ben's cock pushed into him.

Tim's breath whooshed out as he pushed back and sank even lower on the bed. "God, yes." Oh, that was it. So much better than fingers. So much better than anything. He'd missed Ben all night; having him inside was going to take that ache away.

The thrusts came hard and fast, Ben pounding into him.

His hands splaying out for a moment before he could get better purchase, Tim cried out with every thrust. He tried to make words, tried to praise and beg, but all that came were groans and sounds that would let anyone who happened by the window know exactly what was going on. He pushed back, riding hard and getting Ben where he needed him. "Yes, yes, yes. Love you. Harder." There. Those were words.

"Tim. God." Ben pushed harder, hands on his hips, dragging him back into each thrust.

Oh, fuck, yes. Tim let Ben do whatever he wanted, however he wanted to do it. Anything to keep this going, to feel Ben inside him, huge and hard and taking over every single sense. The smell of roses was covered by the scent of sex, and Tim could still taste Ben in his mouth. "Gonna come. Soon, maybe." But not if he could help it.

"Yeah. God." Ben just kept saying it over and over, every thrust harder than the last. "Oh! Love you!" Ben jerked a few more times and then stilled inside him.

Tim gasped, feeling him go. He could feel every twitch, every throb of Ben's cock. "Oh, God." He closed his eyes tightly and reached for his cock, barely getting his fingers around it before he went off like a flare. "*Ben*!"

Ben collapsed down against him, patting his arm. "God."

"I'm sorry I got mad last night," Tim whispered. "I love you. Stay with me tonight?"

"I'm sorry I was a jerk last night. I love you too. I wanna stay." Ben pressed close, even as his cock slipped out.

"Tingling." Tim moaned and twisted a little to get an arm tight around Ben and hold him close. "God, I'm all tingly. That was amazing." He felt raw and used and insanely happy about it. He didn't even care that they needed to move about eight inches to the left to avoid the wet spot. He had clean bedding; they'd get to it later. "I love you."

"I love you, too, Tim. I really do. And you're my top priority, I swear."

"Okay." He petted Ben's arm and nodded. "It's an adjustment, that's all. For all of us. I get that."

"It's worth it, Tim, it is. I'm just used to... going along, you know?" Ben gave him a sloppy kiss. "I'd rather go along with you."

Tim smiled, his heart light. "I like that." He kissed the tip of Ben's nose. "A lot."

"Yeah, me, too." Ben's head rested on his chest, fingers playing idly with his belly.

Tim ran his fingers through Ben's hair, feeling like he was smiling all the way down to his bones. He'd never expected this, not from a routine call to talk to a civilian about suspicious animal deaths. He'd found a lot more than a concerned citizen; he'd found his best friend, and a lover and -- potentially -- a pushy red-headed woman to tease. The case was closed, but Tim's life stretched out in front of him, enticing and sunny. The very best part of it was right there with him, in his arms.

"Good," he whispered. "It's all good, Ben."

It couldn't be better.

Drew Zachary

Printed in the United States
13012 7LV00009B/1/P